THE KRAKEN'S SACRIFICE

A DEAL WITH A DEMON NOVEL

KATEE ROBERT

TRINKETS AND TALES LLC

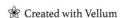

To every person who asked why there wasn't DP in the dragon book...

CONTENT NOTES

B elow, please find all tropes, tags, and CWs for the book. This list was compiled to the best of my knowledge, but may not be exhaustive. Reader discretion is advised.

TROPES: Grumpy/Sunshine, monster romance

TAGS: I'll fuck the brat right out of you, widower, party girl covering up how empty she feels, I got hurt and so I decided emotions are for the birds and I won't feel them anymore, forced proximity, if you don't give me attention I will MAKE you give me attention, auction, tentacles make everything better, orgasms are definitely the proper response to terror, let me teach you how to swim, men will literally lock you in a tower for your own safety instead of going to therapy, he can't just fuck self-confidence into me...but can't hurt to try, prehensile cock

. . .

Content warnings: Abuse/neglect (mental/emotional, parent to child, historical), spousal death (historical, non-graphic, off-page), explicit sex, vomit (non-graphic), pregnancy termination (non-graphic), incidental injuries for magical purposes, grief, body shaming (historical, referenced briefly), reference to age play and to DDlg, slight dollification, use of unconventional gag

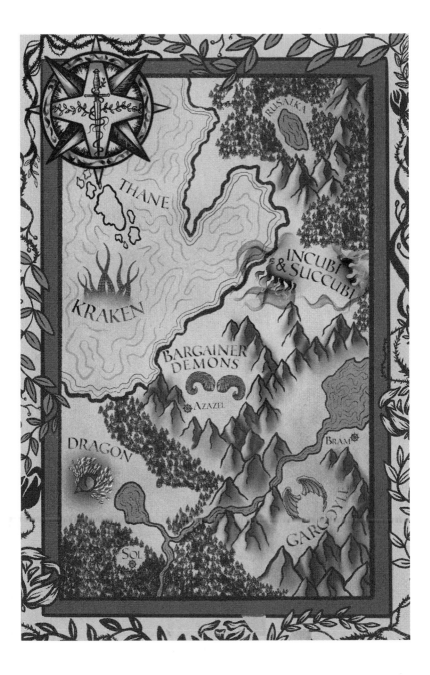

1

CATALINA

"I will ask again. Are you sure?"

I'm not sure what it says about my life that I'm sitting in a sticky booth at a dingy hole-in-the-wall bar staring at a handsome dark-haired white guy. Except, apparently, he's not a guy at all.

Or at least not human.

One would never know he's a demon just by looking at him, but as Azazel turns his head, the light glints strangely off his eyes. A flash of red that sends a shiver down my spine. Not that I'm about to let a little fear dissuade me.

I have nowhere else to go. My family have finally washed their hands of me. My friends are tired of my bullshit and have faded away. But the straw that broke the proverbial camel's back was getting fired last week. I may or may not have been a *tiny* bit behind on my rent, and my landlord says I have to be out by the end of the month.

Tomorrow.

When you're at rock bottom, sometimes the only thing to do is keep digging.

Azazel shifts, and the shadows seem to flicker strangely

around him. They sure as hell aren't following normal patterns in response to the neon lights over the bar. "Catalina."

I jolt. "I'm listening."

"This is of the utmost importance." He leans forward and braces his elbows on the table.

I wince a little, because it's just as sticky as the booth and his suit looks expensive. "Really, you probably shouldn't touch anything in here. You're going to ruin your suit, and, like, I don't know if demons have money, but you'll definitely need to drop a metric shit-ton on dry cleaning."

He sighs, and it takes the wind right out of me. I know that sigh. It's the "Catalina is wasting my time" sigh. I've heard it in countless variations over the years. From my parents, my teachers, my bosses. I am nothing if not consistent.

Catalina, the disappointment.

I clear my throat and work hard to smother the desire to prove I'm exactly the disappointment he already decided I am. Living up to expectations. Or down to them, more specifically.

"I read the contract." I hadn't believed that any of this was real, but at this point, a demon peddling contracts can't be worse than my human options.

Mainly, having to crawl back to my mother and beg her to let me move home. The thought makes my stomach roil. I'll do anything to avoid that outcome. *Anything.* "I accept."

Azazel makes a slight move that's almost a flinch. "If you need more time to think—"

"I don't." I speak too fast, too frantically. It takes effort to inhale slowly and moderate my tone. "I read the contract," I repeat. "I accept the terms."

Seven years of service in the demon realm.

But at the end of it, I get what I most desire.

Mainly, money. Enough that I'll never have to worry about it again, will never be beholden to anyone ever again. I want to spend the rest of my life on a yacht surrounded by beautiful people who will dribble champagne into my mouth and feed me strawberries and tell me I'm pretty. Who will never decide I'm *too much* and withdraw their attention and love. Yeah, I'll have bought that love, but if I've learned one thing, it's that money paves the way to happiness. If that happiness is false and lasts only as long as the money does, who gives a fuck?

The only person who can tell the difference will be me, and I'm happy to close my eyes and pretend.

Azazel looks at me for a long moment, then finally nods. "So be it." A flick of his long fingers, and the contract rolls out across the table in my direction.

All the details are the same as when I last read it. Seven years. I'll serve, but no one can force me into doing something that will harm me. If I become pregnant, I will leave my baby in the demon realm when I return to this one.

I have absolutely no intention of getting pregnant, so that's not an issue.

A pen appears next to the contract, and I don't hesitate. I grab it and scribble out my signature. "Are we going now?"

The contract rolls back up toward him, and he grabs it. He narrows his eyes at me. "Normally, there's more fear and weeping."

He's scary, but he's nowhere near as scary as my mother, who's so cold, she might as well have been carved from ice. It doesn't matter what I do or say, because she won't give me even the smallest reaction. Whether he knows it or not, he's saving me from having to prove her low opinion of me correct. Again.

No use thinking about that. I signed the contract. It's over. Or, more accurately, it's only beginning. Can a demon back out on a signed contract? The thought makes fear flicker for the first time. I clear my throat. "Look, if you get off on that sort of thing, you should have said something from the beginning." I lean forward and widen my eyes. "I'm so scared, Mr. Demon Man. Terrified. Shaking in my boots. Please take pity on me and put me out of my misery."

He rolls his eyes, and a small smile curves his lips. "I take pity on whichever of the territory leaders you end up with. Come along, Catalina." The words aren't unkind, but they contain echoes from past years.

Your poor teachers, having to put up with your recklessness.

Oh, wow, you must be a handful for your girlfriend to deal with.

God, what boy would want to date someone who dances on tables and flirts with everyone who crosses their path?

You, Catalina, are a disappointment.

There's only one way to escape the ghosts in my head, but Azazel takes my hand before I can do more than sweep a look around the bar. It's just as well. For all my bravado, I don't actually know what I'm walking into, and getting sloshed beforehand would be just another mistake in a long line of mistakes.

It's tempting all the same.

The room goes wobbly and transforms to black in a swirling motion that makes me vaguely sick. And then there's a lurch that feels like my guts are actually yanked right out of my body. I open my mouth to scream, but there's no air to draw in.

Is this what dying feels like?

My feet hit the ground hard, almost as if I jumped from a high distance, and I crumple to my knees. "Ouch."

"You didn't pass out. Interesting."

The voice above me still carries the cultured tones of the bargainer demon, but there's a rougher edge to it now. It's deeper too. My head feels like it weighs a thousand pounds, but I manage to lift it and look at the . . . creature . . . standing next to me.

No, not creature. It's Azazel. He may have grown over a foot, gained a bunch of weight in muscle, turned crimson, and sprouted horns, but . . .

Actually that's a lot.

I hiccup. "You really take the demon thing literally, don't you? How very Christian devil of you."

"We came first, Catalina. Where do you think they got the inspiration from?" He sighs, and the sound cuts right through me.

Or maybe that's my stomach suddenly surging. "Az—"

To his credit, he responds quickly. He moves faster than anyone has right to and manages to produce a bucket from somewhere, then shove it under my face just as I throw up. I'm nearly certain I feel his hand rubbing my back, but figure that must be a hallucination.

Azazel may have more use for me than anyone else in my life on account of me signing the contract, but that doesn't mean he really wants me around. And now I'm puking in the hallway.

Typical Catalina.

Sometime later, his low voice penetrates my fog of misery. "It's normal to have side effects from jumping realms. Frankly, I'm impressed you managed not to fall unconscious. Most people do."

I close my eyes and try very hard not to think about how my mouth tastes right now. Surely the demon realm has toothpaste, right? Except I can't focus on that, because

Azazel's pity crawls around beneath my skin, and I'd do anything to claw it free.

I let myself tip back on my ass, effectively breaking the contact with his hand on my back—not a hallucination, apparently—and force a grin. "Oh, please, this has nothing on the time I took a wrong turn and ended up in a biker bar that only served Jack Daniels." Not strictly true. My boyfriend and I had a fight, and he left me on the side of the road, but I'm not about to admit *that*. It's just sad, not entertaining, and I am nothing if I'm not entertaining.

He blinks those eerie dark eyes at me. "What?"

"Bikers only respect like two things—or at least these bikers. I can't pretend to speak for bikers as a community just because I had one interaction with the people at this bar."

Catalina, stop fucking talking.

But I can't. I *never* can. Not when my nerves are strung tight like this. It's not fear. That would be ridiculous. But . . . nerves. "Anyways, those two things are fighting and drinking, and I am a lover not a fighter."

"Catalina—"

I talk right over him, his impatience only driving my words to bubble up faster, spill from my lips as if I can outrace his disappointment. "So I obviously couldn't fight any of them if I wanted to keep my good looks and avoid a hefty hospital bill, which meant the only option was outdrinking every single person in the bar." The memory still makes me shudder. No fear there, of course. Just nerves. "They found me as charming as you do, and I managed to walk out of there with cab fare and only a tiny bit of alcohol poisoning."

I probably should have gone to the hospital, but if I'd done that, they would have called my emergency contact, a.k.a. my mother. Instead, I spent three days on my bathroom floor, wishing for death. Or, if not death, because that's very permanent and I have commitment issues, then a nice little coma that I would wake from feeling refreshed.

"Catalina, *sleep*."

I barely feel the press of Azazel's fingers on my temples before everything goes gray, then fades to black. "Neat trick," I slur.

Even falling into a magical sleep isn't enough to make me miss his irritated sigh.

2

CATALINA

I spend two days recovering in the nicest room I've ever seen. I don't have much choice, seeing as how I've been locked in. Hard not to take that personally, but I'm doing my best to be agreeable, so I try to keep myself occupied in the room itself instead of scheming on ways to break out.

To be fair, the room *is* luxurious. It looks like something out of a movie about what Hollywood people think ye olden days looked like. Giant bed filled with enough blankets to make a comfy burrow. Lush carpets underfoot to cushion the stone floor. Thick curtains on a window overlooking the city.

The city itself looks like an old-school version of cities everywhere. Or maybe even a current one. I'm not a city expert. There are tall buildings and short ones, and I got bored staring at them after the first hour.

Finding out the bathroom had indoor plumbing was a great relief, and the shower is very large, but that only occupied me for a short time too. Same with the wardrobe filled with some of the fanciest clothing I've ever gotten my hands on. All in my size, which is another neat trick. I indulged in a fashion show worthy of any movie montage, but I exhausted the clothes quickly enough.

Azazel appeared briefly to give me a tattoo that apparently functions as a verbal translation spell. Nifty thing, that. There's also a secondary tattoo that apparently marks my demon bargain. But that meeting is far too short for my liking. He obviously doesn't want to spend any more time in my presence than strictly necessary.

Boredom set in quickly.

Food appears at regular intervals, but no matter how much I try to watch the door, I never see the person who brings it. Must be magic, but that knowledge doesn't help me decrease the boredom. It builds and builds inside me, making my skin too tight and my mind staticky.

Azazel locked me up because he didn't want to deal with me. Just like my mother used to. Oh, she called it "grounding," but I'm pretty sure when most kids are grounded, their doors don't have locks on the outside.

I shudder.

"No. Enough of this. I made a bargain with a demon and now I'm entitled to an update," I say aloud. I don't give a fuck that I haven't been hurt and that I've been fed and clothed and nothing has been asked of me. Anything would be better than this. *Anything.*

Which is how I find myself kneeling in front of the lock and trying to pick it. A skill I learned far younger than I'll ever admit . . . and the same one that prompted my mother to install a dead bolt on my door.

"I am not thinking about that right now," I mutter. The bobby pins I pulled from my hair are stronger than most—an expense I justify for this very reason. Having no escape makes me feel like an animal in a trap.

I have no illusions about how far I'll go. I will gnaw off my own limb to escape.

Thankfully, the only thing between me and relative freedom is a locked door. A locked door that seems to be resisting me, but a locked door nonetheless.

"Come on." I twist the pin, feeling for the lever. "Please. I can't stay in here. If I do, I'm going to start screaming and never stop." Dramatic? Yes. Accurate? Also yes.

The lock clicks.

I blink. I hadn't even found the lever yet . . . or at least I didn't think I did. Half-sure I imagined that click, I try the handle.

Unlocked.

"Don't look a gift horse in the mouth, Cat. You're just better than you thought you were." Gods, I don't know what it says that I'm talking to myself, but it's not a good sign. I'm losing it. I need to get out of this room. I push to my feet, take a moment to fix the fall of my dress, open the door, and step into the hall.

"Neat trick."

I scream and practically levitate six feet to the right. A mocking laugh responds. I spin to face the voice and find an unfamiliar bargainer demon. This one is built shorter and more delicate than Azazel—but still plenty tall by human height standards—and they have a second set of horns curving up from their eye sockets. I frown. "Are you a guard?"

"Merely a curious party." They grin. "Name's Ramanu. Pronouns are mostly they/them, but really any will do."

"Nice to meet you." I smooth my hands over my dress, nerves making me want to bounce on my toes. They don't seem dangerous—or at least not more dangerous than anyone else in the world. Worlds? Realms?

I clear my throat. "Are you going to make me go back in my room?"

They seem to study the door, though I don't know exactly how that's possible since they have no actual eyes. "No," they say slowly. "No, I don't think I will. There are a few hours until you're collected for the auction. Want to stretch your legs?"

"Stretch my legs," I echo. I narrow my eyes. "I'm not allowed to wander the halls, am I?"

"Nope." Their grin widens. "But since the castle let you out once, it'll probably do it again, and it's better that you have an escort. Won't stop our fearless leader from popping a blood vessel, but that's just a bonus from where I'm sitting."

I very much want to move, to start down the hall and walk off some of this restless energy, but I don't know if it's a smart idea. Then again, I'm not sure I care. "Do you not like Azazel?"

"It's not a matter of liking Azazel." They turn and offer their elbow. "He's too good at his job. Sometimes it's important to throw a wrench or seven into the gears. Keeps him on his toes."

And I'm a wrench.

No reason for that to sting. I am the problem child, the unruly one, the daughter and girlfriend and employee who can't manage to get anything right. The endless letdown.

That doesn't stop me from slipping my arm through Ramanu's and walking down the hall. I am my most charming version, telling them some of the more outrageous—and harmless—stories about my life and making them laugh. It's pleasant enough, though I can't help feeling their interest is at least partially scrutinizing. Whether that is directed at me specifically or simply because Azazel brought me here is up for grabs.

They stop short and tilt their head to the side. "Well, damn. Duty calls." They slip their arm from mine and squeeze my shoulder. "It was a delight talking with you, Catalina. Take that door, and it should lead you back to your room."

"What door?" I turn to look where they point. *Wait a minute.* I frown. "There wasn't a door there a few seconds ago." I'm not the most observant person, but I would have noticed a door. Especially since the damned hallway has been completely free of them for the duration of our walk.

"The castle shifts as it pleases." They lift their voice. "Please see her back safely."

A chill runs down my spine. "The castle is sentient?"

"Maybe. Maybe not." They shrug. "Doesn't hurt to be polite in any case." They turn and open a door that *definitely* wasn't there a second ago. I catch sight of a short hallway ending in a half-open door.

Azazel's low voice carries down the hall. "Get in here, Ramanu."

Ramanu holds up a single finger to their lips and closes the door softly, leaving me alone. I look up and down my hallway. It's much the same as it's been since we started walking. I turn back to the door they went through and sigh.

It's gone.

The other door really is the only option. If things are moving tonight, then I guess I should put on my best behavior and play obedient human. I'm honestly not sure what that looks like, but I can try.

I grip the door and inhale slowly. "Thanks for letting me out." Like Ramanu said, it doesn't hurt to be polite.

The door doesn't lead back into my room, though. I step

into another hallway. This one feels more official, though I don't know if that's the right word. The one Ramanu and I walked in was very nice, but the walls were mostly plain and the stone was uncovered, whereas thick carpet runs the length of this one. There are paintings here too. They're big and abstract, but the colors draw me in all the same. I could spend hours looking at them.

Best not to.

I keep moving. I have a feeling of being watched, but when I look over my shoulder, there's no one there. Odd. The hallway takes a turn, and I stop short. Stone steps descend into shadows. "Castle, I was nice to you. Please don't lead me into a murder basement."

There's no answer, but I didn't really expect one. I give one last look around, but no doors have magically appeared. Apparently it doesn't matter that I didn't take stairs to get to this point, because I'm taking stairs now.

"Here goes nothing."

I descend for a long time. A *long* time. Until my thighs start to shake and I'm wondering if I should have spent more time in the gym. I don't *hate* the gym, but it's very hard to be surrounded by all those hard and thin bodies when mine is so very average. Not to mention I just flat-out forget to go for weeks—sometimes months—at a time.

"You're mad at me, Castle. Aren't you?" I can't decide if it's particularly unhinged to be talking to a magical castle or just smart. "You've shown me the error of my ways. I'm very sorry for whatever I've done and I'll be good until the auction or whatever is going on. Please take me back to my room."

There's no response. Of course there isn't.

I drag in a breath and keep going. I'm at the point where I'm considering using my dress as a sled and seeing if it's possible to slide down the damned stairs when I turn a corner and reach the bottom.

It's only then that I see the tunnel and the canal running through it. Or maybe it's called something else, but that's the first word that pops into my head. I take a step closer. Now that I'm not fighting for breath and focusing on my shaking thighs, I recognize the scent in the air.

Salt water.

"Why would you have a canal of salt water?" I murmur. Surely it would make more sense to bring fresh water into the city? But then again, this is a magic realm with a magic castle, so maybe they have some other purpose for this tunnel.

That doesn't explain why the castle brought me here, though.

I look up at the dark curve of stone overhead and frown. "I'm *certain* this is not the way back to my room."

A sound in the water has me turning in time to see ripples on the surface . . . as if something large is swimming toward me. *Fast.* I stumble back a step. "Oh god, there's monsters down here, aren't there? You fed me to monsters after I was nice to you!"

But the being who rises from the water isn't a monster. Or isn't *entirely* a monster. They're broad with blue-gray skin that is strangely attractive. Also . . . "You have tentacles."

They stop short. Or their human parts—a well-defined torso and muscled arms and a face with a very cold expression on it—stop short. The tentacles that seem to pass for hair slither around their shoulders, and the bottom half of their body—all tentacles—shifts and lashes out.

"Who are you? A welcome party?" They say it with a sneer of derision. "A single human to meet a king?"

A . . . king.

I've never met a king before. Then again, I've never met a fish-man made of half tentacles either. The smart thing to do is most likely to run, but when presented with the smart thing and the reckless thing, there's really only one option for me.

I tilt my head to the side and make a show of looking him over. "Guess Azazel doesn't think much of you."

His hair tentacles move around his cold face like snakes. I half expect them to hiss at me. Or for him to get pissed. But his expression never wavers. He looks down his crooked nose at me. "Go get your master, human. I don't have time for this."

I eye the mass of tentacles that make up the lower half of his body. It would be very, very easy for him to drag me into the canal and drown me. Pretty sure death by drowning counts as harm, but I still don't really know how the whole demon contract gets enforced, and punishing my murderer is great and all, but I'll be too dead to care.

"Sure," I say slowly. "I'll, uh, go do that now." I back toward the stairs.

Thankfully, the castle hasn't made them vanish in the few minutes since I reached the bottom. Even better, the ascent—which I walk and definitely don't run for my life on —only takes three curves of the staircase before it spits me out into a familiar-looking hallway. "Thanks a lot, Castle."

A door halfway down the hall opens, and I peek inside to find my room. "Oh, thank god. Or thank Castle." I duck inside and shut the door behind me.

Only then do I realize I'm shaking. I knew I was in a different realm, of course. "Toto, we're not in Kansas anymore" and all that. Somehow Ramanu and Azazel didn't ping my monster meter nearly as hard as the kraken king did.

I walk to my bed and flop onto it. "A single human to meet a king." I can't really mimic his deep, icy tones, so I exaggerate the haughtiness. "Someone should meet you with a fucking harpoon. Maybe that would be enough to get the stick out of your ass." Oh well. It doesn't matter if that fishy king got under my skin in record time.

I'll never see him again.

3

THANE

I'm still thinking about the human woman an hour later when I'm led by that blasted demon Ramanu into a large room containing two of the three other territory leaders. Even knowing to expect it, I can't help tensing as I move past them to the inset pool of salt water Azazel has provided. I'm sure the demon knows it's not actually necessary—I hardly dry out after being out of water for only a few hours—but if the other territory leaders underestimate my abilities, I would rather they continue to do so.

Azazel's thoughtfulness makes me suspicious. He's better than his predecessor and shows no inclination to conquer the entire realm, but I'd be a fool to think that isn't a possibility. He's offering a sweet bribe, but I've been around long enough to look for the poison hidden within.

More, I simply don't want to be here.

I have no interest in siring children or taking a partner, even in name. Not after . . .

I shudder and try to cover the involuntary movement. Best not to think of my past, not here while surrounded by predators. To distract myself, I survey the other territory leaders. There's Rusalka, with her indolent smile that doesn't quite hide the potential for violence in every line of her tall body. Bram, the most human-looking of us . . . as long as one doesn't pay attention to the giant wings tucked tight against his body. Or his tail. Or his horns. His long white hair is looking particularly lustrous today. Bastard.

The doors open and Sol stalks through. It takes all my considerable control to remain still as the big dragon passes me. Our territories haven't had a conflict in some time, but old grudges run deep.

It's not his fault Brant's dead. It wasn't his hand that killed my beloved. It wasn't even during one of those conflicts.

But it *was* one of his people who murdered my husband.

"Shall we begin?" Azazel, as always, has impeccable timing. There's a reason the bargainers haven't needed to involve themselves in skirmishes with the other territories recently, and he's it. He's too smooth for my liking, but I can't deny that the entire realm has stabilized since he took over for his people.

Tonight is an extension of that striving for peace. It's entirely possible this whole thing a trap, but I don't think so. The other leaders may waste time chasing their respective tails and trying to prove who's the most dangerous. I don't. I prefer to watch from the depths, weighing their words and actions and considering paths forward. My people are the least in number, and while we can retreat to the deep where none of the others can reach us, if necessary, it's my job to ensure we don't have to make that choice.

Hence my presence here tonight.

I have no need for a human or desire for an heir. I have my heir in the form of my sibling, Embry. As for mating with humans to increase our territory's magic . . . Should

Embry decide that's necessary, that's for zir to plan and enact. Humans are incredibly potent conductors for magic; it's why all the races of this realm and others rushed to procreate with them all those generations ago. A half-human leader would boost our territory's power exponentially. It just won't be *my* child who plays that role.

The lights go low over the main room, and the ones pointing at the short dais brighten, signaling that we're about to begin. *About time.* The others shift as the humans walk through a door and up onto the dais. I don't have much experience with humans as a whole, but best I can tell, they all seem to be fine specimens of their people.

"Make your choices," Azazel says softly.

I barely listen as the others claim their prizes. I recognize one of these sacrifices to Azazel's ambition; the soft brunette who mouthed off when I arrived. I narrow my eyes. What game is the demon playing? Are these more than the peace offering he claims? What other reason would he have to send one as a welcome, even if it was one I found wanting?

It doesn't make sense. I could have snapped her neck. Drowned her. Hurt her in a thousand different ways. While claiming a human from this auction will require a demon bargain, I'm under no such geas now.

No, he didn't send her. He wouldn't risk such a valuable piece of his plan. Which begs the question . . . Why was she there?

Azazel turns and looks in my direction. It's only then that I realize Bram and Rusalka have chosen their humans; there's only Sol and I left. I exchange a look with him, but he doesn't immediately speak. Ceding the final choice to me. It would be so much easier to hate the dragon if he wasn't so damned conscientious.

My human is still left.

What am I thinking? She's not mine. She never will be. The smart thing to do would be to choose the other, to avoid strange thoughts like that. *She* is dressed in white and has fetching bright red hair. She's also trembling, just a little. Not enough that it's visible, but I am uniquely tuned to water, and what are humans if not water based? She's terrified.

My human isn't scared. She's clothed—if one can call wearing that scrap of dress "clothed"—in a deep blue that makes me think of home. It hugs her curves, showing off a body that had been mostly hidden when I saw her earlier. "Blue," I find myself saying.

Sol's shoulders drop the tiniest bit—in relief?—and he claims the one in white. Then it's over. Things happen quickly after that. The women are brought off the dais to their respective territory leaders, and the pairs are in turn escorted to a series of doors that have appeared around the perimeter of the room.

I hold ours open for my human without thinking. She's watching me with a strange emotion, but it doesn't feel like fear. That's a relief. I have little time for fear; comfort is not one of my skill sets.

The room we find ourselves in is small and unadorned. I inhale deeply. The humidity in here is significantly higher than it was in the greater room. It's an effort not to roll my eyes. Azazel is laying it on too thick. It would take days for most of my people to reach a danger point. Over a week for me, because of my inherent magic as king. Truly, he's just showing off.

"I'm surprised you picked me." She says it so matter-of-factly, it takes me a moment to register the words. By that time, the woman has turned away to stare at the rivulets of water that begin coursing down the stone walls. I don't see the small divot form at the bottom to catch the water, but it's there by the time I look down.

She looks back at me, a frown forming between her dark brows. She's very attractive. She's got a softness that I find intriguing despite myself. It doesn't matter. She'll be well taken care of, and I won't see much of her after we travel back to my territory. I'm sure some of my informal court will find her attractive as well. She'll have no shortage of partners should she desire them.

"Why did you pick me?"

I look away. "You're all the same to me. One human is as good as another."

Her breath hitches, but when I look back, she's smiling at me. I shift back before I realize what I'm doing. There is something *wrong* with that smile. And it's not an overt threat, but there's a shine to her eyes that makes my tentacles twitch in warning. "Stop that."

"Stop what?" She takes a step closer to me. "I'm not doing anything."

"Yes, you are, and I don't like it."

"You don't have to be scared of me, King Kraken. I don't even like sushi."

My brain skips. "You don't like—"

She opens her mouth, no doubt to deliver another confounding and irritating statement, but the door opens before she can say something else. Azazel walks through and raises his brows. "Do we have a problem?"

"Not at all." The dangerous shine in her eyes melts away as if it were never there, and she laces her hands before her, the very picture of obedience.

I don't trust it for a moment.

"Azazel . . ." I'm not certain what I mean to say. I can't be the only territory leader to leave this auction without a human in tow. Our realm is at peace for the time being, but that doesn't change the fact conflict is as certain as the tide. None of us reached our positions without cost, and each of us would start a war in a heartbeat if we thought it would benefit our people.

He moves deeper into the room, and I turn to find a desk has appeared. The demon circles it and sinks behind it. He rolls out a contract. "The terms, as agreed."

"You'll forgive me if I read it over one last time before signing."

His mouth tightens. "A bargain is sacred."

Of that I have no doubt. Just like I have no doubt Azazel is capable of plenty of underhanded behavior when it suits him. "All the same."

He sighs and shoves the contract at me.

It takes several long moments to read it over, and I am achingly aware of the human the entire time. She shifts from foot to foot, swings her hands back and forth, and finally starts humming under her breath.

"Cease your fidgeting," I snap. "You're worse than a child."

She instantly goes still. Again, something like guilt flares. I don't know how to be around new people any longer, how to learn to ride the tides of their emotions. Losing Brant stole any softness I was capable of. My sibling has grown accustomed to my sharp edges and cold retreats, but this human hasn't. I don't know what prompted her into making a deal with Azazel, but surely I can make even the smallest effort to be kind.

Seven years is a long time to share a space, even if I have no intention of spending more time with her than strictly necessary.

But when I look at her, she has that wild smile firmly in place. It's the only warning I get before she speaks, her voice honeyed. "If you were into age play, you should have just said something. Shall I call you *daddy*?"

"No." The word comes out too sharp, but she's set me back again, and I don't know how to deal with this. "Do not, under any circumstances, call me that."

She parts her lips, but Azazel cuts in. "That was a hard boundary, Catalina. Respect it."

Catalina.

A pretty name for a pretty human. Even the way she scrunches her nose at him is pretty. "You're definitely a Daddy."

"Catalina." There's a hint of warning in the demon's tone. "Do not test me."

"I live to test you." Her smile goes sweet. "But I'll be good. I promise."

"I don't believe that for a moment." He turns to me. "I don't think this is a good pairing. Give me a few days, and I'll find you a suitable replacement."

"No." I don't know why I say it. In the short time I've associated with this woman, she's more than proven herself to be a catastrophe in waiting. She will create waves in my carefully balanced life, and that is the last thing I want.

But I don't miss the way her shoulders dip the tiniest bit at his offer. Resignation. That's the emotion. As if Azazel's words confirmed something she already knew. It's a direct counterpoint to her previous cheer that bordered on animosity.

"Are you sure?" Azazel watches me closely. "If she is harmed, your territory is forfeit."

"I'm aware," I say slowly. "I chose her. I'll keep her." I set the contract on the desk and sign before he can offer again.

The contract itself is nothing more than I expected. Azazel laid out the terms in his invitation. No harm is to come to the human, and while the respective leaders can attempt to seduce their prizes, they cannot force—by any definition of the word—the woman into bed with themselves or any others. Violation of the contract results in our territories being forfeit, a hefty price the others are willing to risk for the chance to boost their territory's health with half-human offspring.

Easy enough to agree to.

I have no intention of touching this woman, and I certainly will not be breeding her. I have my heir. I will not compromise Embry's future rule. Should ze want to mate with a human once ze takes the throne, that is zir choice.

Azazel frowns down at my signature and then turns that frown on Catalina. "I have reservations about this pairing."

"Of course you do." She's swifter than I anticipate, plucking the pen from my hand, then scrawling out a signature above her name, spelled in English.

It's done.

Azazel sighs. "Do not give me reason to regret this."

"No promises," Catalina sings.

I am suddenly sure *I'm* the one who's going to regret this.

4

CATALINA

I don't know why I'm surprised King Kraken takes me down to the canal where I first met him. I pause at the bottom of the stairs. "Pretty sure drowning translates as harm."

He gives me a look. Or at least I think it's a look. His expression hasn't shifted from the cold mask he's worn from the moment I caught sight of him in the room where we were auctioned off. If auctioning off is even accurate. There was no haggling, no rising bids. They just called out a color and claimed that woman.

I don't know why the kraken chose me. He doesn't like me. It's written all over the derisive way he talks to me and the blatant distance he keeps between us. I read the contract. I know he can seduce me, but he doesn't seem interested in doing any kind of seducing.

That should be a relief. I won't pretend I'm not more than a little curious about the tentacles—truly, I've seen some inspired art in my day, and the possibility of experiencing it in real life is more tantalizing than I expected—but that doesn't mean I want to fuck a fish. Wait. Krakens are squid, right? I'm pretty sure squid aren't technically classified as fish. I frown and then shrug. Oh well, it doesn't matter. His obvious distaste for me echoes far too many people in my life.

Even the tentacle-man doesn't want me.

Truly, I just keep digging past rock bottom, deeper and deeper. I would have thought making a deal with a demon would be the worst of it, but apparently, I was not imaginative enough when it comes to disappointing those around me.

"I am not drowning you."

I will never admit it out loud, but his voice is nice. It's deep enough that I'd be drawn to him if not for the damned cold that permeates every aspect of his presentation. He holds out a hand, and for all that, there's no invitation here, just a clear command for me to take it.

Now isn't the time to fight for the sake of fighting. Azazel promised my safety, and while I don't think he likes me very much, he's painfully serious about the bargain itself. He won't let King Kraken hurt me, especially not in Azazel's own castle.

"What's your name?"

He blinks. "Excuse me?"

"Your name. I'm assuming you have one." I tried to decipher it on the contract itself, but it was an incomprehensible scribble that would do any doctor proud. "Unless you want me to keep calling you King Kraken."

For a moment, it seems like he might not answer me, but he finally sighs. "Thane."

Damn it. It's a nice name. Not that it matters. I know my strengths, which are few, and my weaknesses, which are plentiful. If there's one thing I'm going to do, it's shatter myself against the wall of someone who will always find me wanting.

I manage to keep my silence as I slip my hand into his and follow him into the water. It doesn't escape my notice that he keeps his tentacles from touching me, despite the fact I'm walking at his side and they are a mass around both of us. But why would he want to touch me more than he strictly has to? He doesn't like me.

The water hits my thighs and the hem of my short dress. We keep going. The canal is deeper than I realized, and I'm quickly soaked to the chest. "Um."

Thane pauses. "Yes?" he grits out.

"I suppose now is a good time to tell you that I don't know how to swim."

The first flash of emotion warms his face. Complete disbelief. "You don't know how to swim," he echoes. "How is that possible?"

My mother found public pools to be filthy and refused to let me swim in them. The same could be said for lakes, rivers, and the ocean itself, not that I had much reason to spend time in any body of water. "Just lucky, I guess."

He's still staring at me like I sprouted a second head, which is hilarious considering what's sprouting from *his* head. Thane eyes the water and then me again. "This presents a complication."

No shit, Sherlock.

"Does it?" I ask sweetly. "Are you sure you weren't going to drown me? Because even if I could swim, I sure as hell can't breathe underwater."

Another of those pauses that speaks volumes. Thane shakes his head slowly. "Right. Of course. An oversight on my part. We'll speak with—"

"Is there a problem?"

We turn to find Ramanu leaning against the wall near

the stairs. They're relaxed, as if they've been there for hours, and I can't tell if they sprinted here or simply materialized, courtesy of the castle. Either way, I'm relieved to see a friendly face, even if I only spoke to them briefly today. "Ramanu!"

"No problem, demon." It seems impossible, but Thane has gone even colder.

Ramanu grins, and I recognize that expression down to my very soul. This is another person who likes ruffling feathers. They lift their hand, and Thane stares at the bracelet dangling from their black claws. "Where did you get that?"

"I'm a bargainer demon." Ramanu swings the bracelet idly. "We make bargains."

"That doesn't belong to you."

"It does now." Their grin never wavers. "What will you give me for it?"

For one wild moment, I think Thane really considers giving *me* for the bracelet. I'm honestly not entirely opposed to the idea. Ramanu seems like fun, and they actually emote, which would be a nice change of pace from this icy kraken.

Thane shakes his head sharply. "You want something. Stop playing games and state your offer."

"Spoilsport." Ramanu pouts. "Fine. You will grant me access to your keep to check on your pretty human."

Thane narrows his eyes. "That was already in the contract."

"Yes, it was." Ramanu twirls the bracelet. "But I want solo check-ins with the human."

If they were anyone else, I would think they were insinuating they want sex, but Ramanu is so focused on Thane, I get the feeling this little power play has nothing to do with me. Because why would it? I'm a newcomer to this realm, and beyond that, I'm only here because Azazel needed another pawn to move around his chessboard. I matter less than his endgame, than Thane's endgame, and apparently even than Ramanu's endgame.

Thane finally nods. "Deal."

"Goddess, you didn't even haggle." Ramanu tosses the bracelet, and Thane grabs it out of the air with one of his tentacles. The demon looks at me, or at least turns in my direction. "I can't speak to the quality of the company, but you're safe with this stick-in-the-mud. I'll come around in a week and check on you." They grin. "Try not to wander your way into a watery grave in the meantime."

We watch Ramanu push off the wall and stride gracefully to the stairs. Within seconds, they're gone, leaving us alone once again. I stare after them for several beats, but I quickly grow bored of trying not to look at Thane. Also, the water is chilly, and I'm fighting not to wrap my arms around myself.

Thane is staring at the bracelet with the strangest expression on his face. It's almost like loss. He shuts it down the moment he realizes I'm watching and shifts the tentacle with the bracelet closer to me. "Put this on."

I make no move to grab it. "What is it?"

"Humans used to be more common in this realm. There were those among my people who had—have a vested interest in not drowning those humans. They create these." He shakes the bracelet at me again. "This is spelled to allow you to breathe underwater."

Shock makes me forget to be snarky. "Is that possible?"

"It won't help with your inability to swim, but you won't die as you flounder."

The sharp words snap me back into myself. This isn't a

gift. Not really. It's a way of protecting his investment. I could stand here and keep arguing, or I can take the damned bracelet and let him get me back to his home.

Oh god, am I going to live underwater? Even if I won't drown, surely I'll freeze over time? Or at least wrinkle into a prune of a person?

I pluck the bracelet from his tentacle before I can think better of it and shove it onto my right wrist. "There. Happy?"

"I'm never happy, human."

He sounds far too severe for that to be a joke. I don't get a chance to question further, though, because he moves in a surge. His tentacles twist and squirm around my waist, far more strongly than I expected. I barely have time to gasp when he dives into the canal, taking me with him.

The water closes over my head, but we keep descending. I stare up, watching the light above us blink away. I instinctively hold my breath, but that only lasts until the first time Thane's tentacles shift around my waist. It feels strange, and I gasp . . . inhaling water.

Or at least I *should* be inhaling water.

Instead, it feels just like air. Salty air, but breathable all the same. Magic. This whole damned world is magic. There's no point in fighting Thane's movements, so I let myself go limp. It's . . . peaceful. I can't hear anything but the soft sounds of us cutting through the water, can't see anything but shadows, am completely buoyed by a strange weightlessness even as I'm dragged along.

I don't notice the shift in color first; it's the change in temperature I register before anything else. Warmth starts to seep into my bones until the water around me is almost balmy. The light has morphed as well, going from near black to blue and then turquoise.

Then I see the fish.

I gasp, bubbles erupting from my lips. I've never seen fish like this before. They're bright and strange and don't seem the least bit bothered by the predator in their midst. They flit and flicker around us in vibrant groups. It's beautiful.

Thane doesn't give me the opportunity to revel in the magic of the moment. He tows me up and up and up. My head goes a little funny, but I don't have a chance to think too hard about it as he surges out of the water and onto a rock platform. He deposits me there, unceremoniously dumping me on the ground.

By the time I get to my hands and knees, he's already moving toward a wide staircase leading up. I blink blearily. "Hold on." The sensation in my head gets stronger. What the hell is wrong with me? It's been a long day, and there is the whole "auctioned to a tentacle-man" that I need to process at some point, but I feel awful.

"Stop wasting time."

I look up to find him back in front of me. He's beautiful in the way that glaciers are beautiful. You'll definitely freeze your ass off if you get too close, but it's pretty and harsh and unforgiving, which draws you in all the same. The gray-blue of his skin makes him look at home in this rocky place with reflections of the water playing over the walls and ceiling.

The last thing I want is to stand right now, with my ears ringing like I just went three rounds with someone far more proficient at boxing than I am. But I can't kneel here at his feet while he looks at me like I'm some piece of garbage that washed ashore.

I fight my way to my feet. My stomach threatens to rebel, but I haven't eaten anything today, so there's nothing to purge. I look up, up, up into Thane's inky eyes. "Happy now?"

"No."

"Yeah, didn't think so." I press the heel of my hand to my temple. "You seem like the type who's happiest when you're miserable. It'd be charming if it weren't so annoying."

"Listen, human—"

But I'm not listening. My brain goes strange, and the room takes a sickening tinge and feels like it's moving even though my feet are planted on bare stone. "I think I'm going to pass out." I sound remarkably normal, as if commenting on the weather.

"Excuse me?"

I part my lips to answer, but everything goes gray, and my knees give out. I expect the sharp sensation of my head cracking on the rock—it's going to hurt like a bitch—but it never comes.

The last thing I feel before darkness takes me is a mass of tentacles creating a soft cradle for my body.

5

THANE

"What were you *thinking*?"

I cross my arms over my chest and try not to get defensive. It's nearly impossible when faced with two accusing pairs of eyes pointed in my direction. "It didn't occur to me that it could be a problem."

"She's *human*, you fool." Azazel flexes his fists like he wants to slam one into my face. "They aren't like us. They especially aren't like you."

"We don't have as many humans in our territory as you do," Embry cuts in. No one looking at us would mistake zir and me for anything other than siblings, for all that Embry inherited our mother's more green-based tones. Ze and I both got our father's crooked nose, which ze is looking down right now. "Honestly, Thane, he's right. What were you thinking?"

"I wasn't—"

"I think *that* is abundantly clear."

"Enough, Azazel. We both know this wasn't intentional." There's no relief to be had in Embry's defense, though, because ze points a finger at me. "But you should have asked for more details before bringing her back through the canal."

"It's the quickest way home." That's the only thing I was thinking about.

No, that's a lie. It wasn't the only thing I was thinking about it. I couldn't get the sight of Brant's bracelet in Ramanu's hands out of my head. We may not have many humans, or the like, in our territory these days, but the bracelets were always in high demand before among people who wanted to play tourist in their respective rivers and lakes. Especially parents of children who lived close to bodies of water. The assurance that they wouldn't drown was worth its weight in gold.

Not that Brant ever charged enough for the bracelets.

Seeing Ramanu holding one of them, knowing the demon possibly even got it from Brant himself, felt like a slap in the face. I couldn't think beyond the need to reclaim the item and get out of the castle as quickly as possible. The deep path is the fastest, so that's the one I took.

It never occurred to me that it could hurt Catalina.

I glance at the bed. She levitates over it, wrapped in a bubble of magic that Embry assures me is proven to help humans with this particular sickness.

A sickness I caused with my carelessness.

"They can't adjust to depth changes as quickly as we can. If you take her deep, you have to ease her back to the surface." Embry swirls zir fingers through the air, eyes narrowed as ze considers Catalina. "She'll be fine."

"This time." Azazel still looks like he wants to beat my face in. I don't blame him. I made a mistake—a costly one. He glares. "No one can argue this isn't harm. I'd be well within my rights to call this contract null and void."

I tense. If he does that, I'll lose the territory to him. I'll lose *Embry's* territory to him. The thought leaves me sick to my stomach. "I meant her no harm."

"Intentions matter less than the result. You caused harm, no matter what you meant to do."

"I know. I'm sorry."

"Someone get the record books, Thane has apologized." The raspy quip makes us all look at the bed. Catalina has her eyes cracked. She still looks too pale and almost frail, but she must be feeling better if she can mouth off.

Azazel is at her side in an instant. "I apologize, Catalina. I didn't realize Thane's intentions to travel the way he did, or I would have educated him on the dangers involved for you."

She looks at him, and there's something wary in her hazel eyes that makes me want to shift between Azazel and her. It doesn't make any sense. If anything, she should be looking to the demon for protection from *me*. Azazel is a fearsome leader, but he has a reputation for taking great care with his humans. Surely she must know that, or she wouldn't have entered into the bargain with him in the first place.

Catalina blinks, and the moment passes. "I'm fine. No harm done."

"I disagree," he growls.

"Well, it doesn't really matter if you agree or not, does it? Now be a good demon daddy and tell Thane you're not going to take his territory over a simple misunderstanding."

Embry's eyes are far too wide as ze takes in the human. "Catalina—"

"A simple mistake," Catalina says firmly. It doesn't seem to matter that she's flat on her back in a room filled with three beings bigger and stronger than her. There's not even a waver there.

Something akin to admiration flares inside me. I don't understand this woman, and frankly, I find her borderline abrasive in the short time we've known each other, but she's no coward.

Azazel curses softly. "I promised you safety, Catalina."

"There are no guarantees in this world, just like there are no guarantees in mine." She smiles a little. "Thanks for riding to my rescue like a horny knight in shining armor, but I'm perfectly fine."

She's lying through her teeth. Oh, it's not there in her voice or her placid expression, but I can feel it in her body all the same. She's not fine, for all that she wants us to believe it. But *why?* What motivation could she possibly have to lie for me? If the contract is broken, Azazel will sweep her back to the castle and spend the next seven years ensuring she wants for nothing to make up for it. He's a bastard, but he's a fair one.

Azazel finally nods. "Should anything change—"

"It won't."

He turns to me. "No more mistakes, Thane."

"You have my word." I didn't intend to be careless with her, but Azazel is right. Intentions matter little where harm is concerned. "It won't happen again."

"See that it doesn't." He stalks to the door and disappears through it. I feel the moment he leaves my keep through a portal of his making. It's a disturbance in the air, there and gone in a moment.

"Let's get you down." Embry guides the bubble of healing magic down to the bed. "You should stay inside it for a few minutes or so, though. The spell will fade then, and you'll be free to move about. I believe you're fine now, but I would prefer to err on the side of caution."

"Okay." Catalina's smile goes a bit soft and far more real

than I've seen in our short acquaintance. "I promise to be good and lie here until the spell ends." She makes a face. "Spells. I don't know why that's what trips me up about this whole experience, but it's very strange."

"You've had some big shocks." Embry smiles down at her. "Try to take it easy and give yourself some space to adjust."

Embry always was better with this sort of thing than I am. Ze knows exactly the right things to say and, most importantly, ze genuinely cares. Ze will be a great leader when I step down.

Exhaustion weighs on me. I never wanted to lead. Being the eldest sibling put me in that position, and I did my duty as tradition demanded. I knew the cost would be great, but I never reckoned on losing nearly everything. What point is there in a throne when the person I loved most in this world is gone?

Grief is a strange thing. Some moments, even years later, the loss of Brant is enough to make me feel like I'll never breathe again. But yesterday, I realized I can't remember the exact angle of his smile. Time may heal most wounds, but the cost of that healing is more than I'm comfortable paying.

I don't want to do this, to play caretaker to this human with the entirety of the territory hanging in the balance. But stepping down now means dumping this whole mess in Embry's lap, and I won't do that to zir.

"I'll take it from here," I say softly.

Ze looks at me askance but shrugs. "Try not to upset her."

I don't know if that's possible. This strange woman has managed to confound me several times during our short acquaintance. I can't imagine I'm going to suddenly become better at interpersonal communication in the next three minutes. "I won't."

Embry hesitates but finally shakes zir head and leaves the room. With zir gone, there's no one to look at except the human on the bed. Catalina has her eyes closed, which should be a welcome relief, but without her staring me down with that wild look in her eyes, she seems . . . smaller.

"I'm sorry."

"It would be a shame to lose your kingdom on the first day." She says it so carelessly, as if her life matters so little.

It shouldn't bother me. I don't know this woman. She's nothing to me, and my people matter far more than one human life. And yet . . . "I have no wish to harm you." That's not good enough, though. I've almost killed her. Surely I can give a little more explanation as to why I was so careless. "Being around the other territory leaders is challenging for me. It wasn't very long ago that we were in open conflict with each other, and Sol—"

She opens her eyes. "The dragon."

"How do you know that?" We were only in the main room with the group for a brief encounter, and no one spoke.

"Lucky guess." She closes her eyes again. "You went out of your way to keep more distance between you and the dragon than you did with any of the others."

She noticed that?

I move closer to the bed despite myself. Really, Catalina is quite fetching for a human. She's soft and pale with lovely dark hair. Her lips are also . . . No. Best not to think about her lips. I clear my throat. "One of his people killed my husband five years ago. The bracelet on your wrist was made by him, the last one he made if I'm not mistaken."

"*What?*" Her eyes fly open. "Oh, Thane, I'm so sorry."

I wave that away. I can't stand pity. Enough of my people have it lingering in their eyes when they look at me. Escaping Brant's loss is impossible, but the weight of it seems to increase the more time I spend in others' presences. Embry is the exception, but ze is the person I'm closest to in this world. Ze knows the last thing I want is pity. "It was a long time ago, but Ramanu holding it made me forget myself."

"Five years is both a long time and no time at all." Something in her voice speaks to experience, but it's flavored differently. She didn't lose someone, but she lost . . . something. I'm tempted to ask, but I don't want to give her a false sense of what this is.

"Yes," I say simply.

"I don't want kids."

I blink at the sudden change in subject. "Excuse me?"

"Kids. There's a clause in the contract that says if I get knocked up, my kid stays here." She carefully sits up as the bubble of magic dissolves around her. "I don't want to be pregnant. I had a shit show of a mother as an example and can't guarantee I won't fuck up a kid the same way she fucked up me. It's not worth the risk. I won't do it."

There's none of her defiant joy in the bleak words. Once again, I can only meet her honesty with honesty. "I don't want children either. I never have. Embry is my heir, and I'll do nothing to compromise zir position."

Catalina narrows her eyes. "Then why is that even in my contract? Or is that a bargainer-specific thing?"

"The territories get their strength from their leaders. Our magic has been faltering in recent generations, and procreating with a human will provide a boost since humans are excellent conductors for magic. The other territory leaders no doubt intend to breed with their respective humans and create heirs that way."

"That's very nondemocratic of them. Are they all monarchies like you?"

It's a mistake to linger in this room longer than strictly necessary. As we talk, the strength comes back into her voice, and she scoots to the edge of the bed, causing her dress to ride up to an indecent height. She doesn't seem to notice, so I do my best to keep my gaze firmly above her shoulders.

I'm only partially successful. I make it to her chest, but each motion she makes has her breasts straining precariously against the fabric of her dress. Her generous curves look one tiny tug from bursting free.

To distract myself, I answer her question. "No. The incubi and succubi don't follow bloodlines for who takes the leadership position. Rusalka likely intends to use some of her chosen warriors to breed with the human."

"Kinky." Catalina smiles slowly, life sparking back onto her pretty face. "Do you think they'll line up and run a train on her? I only met her briefly, but she seems like she enjoys having a good time, and that sounds like a *good time*."

"Is that something you'd be interested in?" I don't know what possesses me to ask such an inappropriate question, but it slips free before my brain catches up with my mouth.

"Me?" She carefully gets to her feet. Without thinking, I move my tentacles out of the way as she steps closer. Her grin widens, and that strange look flares in her hazel eyes. Catalina reaches out and presses her hands to my bare chest. She meets my gaze, her touch scorching me. "I'm more interested in tentacles."

I don't understand why I lean toward her in response. She is infuriating and nothing like any partner I've had in the past. She's certainly nothing like Brant. His charm was sunny and without the wild edge that lurks in the curve of her full lips. And yet . . . she draws me all the same.

It's a feel beyond reason, beyond logic. That should be enough to make me turn around and leave the room and never look back. I even go so far as to silently command my body to do exactly that.

But I don't leave.

Instead, I stand there and wait to see what she'll do next.

6

CATALINA

There's something wrong with me. I've been told this enough times over the course of my life to start to believe it. In this moment, there's no other explanation for the fact I'm sidling up to a man with blue-gray skin and tentacles. I half expect his skin to be clammy, but it's cool and pleasant. It almost feels a little rubbery, but not in a bad way.

"I almost killed you." His voice is low and cold, but at least he's still talking to me.

If I were smart, I'd use his obvious guilt as leverage for a bargain just between us. One that involves getting whatever I might possibly want to make the next seven years in this place tolerable.

But I established a long time ago that I'm not smart.

"You could make it up to me." I stare into his face, all hard lines that stop him from being anything as tame as *pretty*. He's as harsh as the ocean itself. His eyes are inky black, but they're not emotionless. Not when he's staring at my mouth in something like agony.

The Kraken King wants me.

The thought thrills me, which only confirms that I really am a fool. I wet my lips, and he follows the movement, his whole body tensing in a way that sends a thrill down my spine.

"How?" He clears his throat, and when he speaks again, his voice is lower. Rougher. "How would you like me to make it up to you, Catalina?"

Turn back.

Turn back now!

I ignore the little voice inside me. "Will you give me your tentacles, Thane? Make me feel good?" I don't know why it feels safer to ask for them than his cock, but it does. I meant what I said about not having kids, and while I'm on the pill, none of my stuff made the transfer with me to the demon realm, so I'm not protected right now. Reckless as I may be, even I have lines.

"You want sex." His voice gets colder even as his eyes go hot. "I almost killed you, and now you want orgasms."

It takes far more effort than I'll ever admit to shrug as if I'm not holding my breath. "Seems a fair trade."

For a moment, I'm sure he'll tell me to fuck right off with that twisted logic. I almost hope he does. It *is* twisted. He doesn't mean me harm—of that I'm sure—but that's a long way from caring about me. Thane obviously doesn't. He doesn't even like me.

It only makes me want him more.

I know it will hurt in the end. It always does. The knowledge has never stopped me before, and it's not going to stop me now. "What do you say?"

"If you want me to stop, say stop."

I barely have time to process his words before he moves. Or, rather, his tentacles move. They surge up my legs and catch the hem of my dress. One jerk from either side, and they rip it right up the center. It was too tight to wear anything underneath, so there's not a single scrap of fabric to protect me from the intensity of Thane's stare.

He wraps a tentacle around my waist and lifts me before moving us both toward the bed. Once again, he keeps a careful distance between us, standing at the edge of the bed as his tentacles slide over my body. They circle my wrists and tug them over my head to pin me against the mattress. Two more tentacles wrap around my thighs and press them wide.

Gentle. He's so damned gentle with me. It doesn't matter. I pull on his hold, and I might as well try to fight against iron for all I can move.

Desire surges, so strong that it takes my breath away. "That's a start."

His brow furrows. "You talk too much."

I ignore the sting of the statement. Mostly. "That's only because you're not doing your job properly. Otherwise I wouldn't be able to talk at all." I take a breath to keep going but moan when the tips of two tentacles prod at my pussy.

He parts me, and as exposed as I feel right now, I can't stop looking at his face as he stares at the apex of my thighs. Thane looks . . . tormented.

That's new. Normally when I take partners to bed, they're enthusiastic or withdrawn, but I've never been looked at like I'm the source of every irritation in their lives and yet they can't stop themselves from touching me. It's a heady thing, even as it hurts a little.

Thane chose me for the bargain. He turned down Azazel's offer to change me out. He took the barest invitation from me and ripped off my clothes and spread me out like his own personal buffet.

I don't know why he's acting like he doesn't want this.

There's no opportunity to ask, though. Not with him pressing one tentacle into me. It doesn't feel like anything I've experienced before. It's not hard like a cock or fingers or a dildo. It's certainly not warm and wet like a mouth, though a tongue is the closest comparison I can find. Even if the texture isn't quite right. His tentacle is cool and almost fluid as he explores the inside of me.

God, that feels good. Really good.

I try to keep my eyes open to watch his expression, to drink in the utter concentration on his face. It doesn't matter if he seems conflicted. He's doing what I asked and making me feel good. And he's doing it *well* too.

The tentacle inside me twists, and I cry out. Thane freezes. "Good?"

"Good," I gasp. "Keep doing that."

After a beat, he resumes the movement. Twisting and twisting. I distantly register that he's feeding me more of his tentacle, filling me almost uncomfortably, but I can't think past the pleasure pounding through me in time with the beat of my heart. Is he using *suckers* down there? Is that what the steady pulsing is inside me? It's so good, and yet, even as it builds, I'm not certain I can get there. "My clit. I need you to touch my clit."

He hesitates. I have the hysterical thought that I'm going to have to teach this kraken what a clitoris is, but Thane doesn't give me a chance to. Another tentacle slithers around my waist and down my stomach to my clit. He gives me an almost-tentative stroke, and then his expression goes hard. "Beg for it."

I almost do. Almost. But I am who I am, and I've never submitted easily once in my life. "Make me."

The tentacle reverses course. I cry out in protest, and he takes that opportunity to shove a different tentacle into my mouth. It doesn't penetrate far. It certainly doesn't hurt, but it shocks me all the same. He's faintly salty on my tongue, his tentacles covered in the same vaguely rubbery skin as his torso. One of the small suckers pulls at my tongue, and I moan.

"It will feel even better on your clit." The rough edge to his cold voice is the only indication that he's affected by what he's doing to me. He gives my tongue one last suck and eases his tentacle from my mouth.

I'll fight him later. I need this too much right now. Words bubble up and escape so fast that they tumble over each other as they leave my lips. "Please. My clit. Do that to my clit. Make me cum. *Please.*"

He watches me for several beats even as he continues fucking me with one tentacle. I open my mouth to keep begging, but it ends up not being necessary. The tentacle he had in my mouth courses down my body. This time, there's no hesitation as it slides against my heated flesh. I register that it slides better now that it's wet with my spit and almost cum on the spot. "Thane!"

"Give it to me," he snaps.

My brain wants to deny him for the sake of denying him. My body has other ideas. He twists one last time inside me and presses one of his suckers to my clit. It feels like a bomb goes off inside me. I scream, and my back bows as the entire room devolves into static. I've orgasmed before, of course. I've orgasmed *a lot.*

None of those past ones compare to this.

I think I actually black out a little. I'm vaguely aware of him easing out of me and pulling back the covers on the bed so he can tuck me in. All without touching me with his hands. I actually reach for him before I remember myself and let my hand drop to the bed.

"Consider us even, Catalina." His voice still has that extra rasp of desire.

I watch him cross the room, but he bypasses the door. It's only then that I realize there's a pool in the corner of the room. Thane slips into it and disappears beneath the water. He doesn't look back once.

All I want to do is sleep, but I struggle out of the comfortable bed and stumble to the edge of the pool. It's an irregular shape that makes me wonder if it was carved out of the floor or if it's a natural occurrence. I go to one knee and touch the water. It's not freezing, but it's definitely not a hot spring. The water is the same vaguely balmy temperature that I registered before Thane surfaced. It's also clear. I peer down into it. There are several divots that might be for sitting or lounging, but the part that catches and holds my attention is the hole in the center descending into darkness.

That's where Thane went.

I sit cross-legged and stare at it for a very long time. It makes sense that a place built for people who are part fish would have watery ways to move around. We're on land, technically, but that doesn't make much difference. I bet a lot of this place is actually underwater. Thane doesn't seem to need to breathe air, so maybe he doesn't surface often.

My bracelet catches my eye. It allows me to breathe underwater. Before I can talk myself out of it, I slip into the water. I take a breath and then submerge myself. It takes fifteen seconds for my instincts to start screaming that I need to get to the surface. Even braced on one of the under-water shelves, I'm achingly aware of that dark hole and what might come out of it.

If it connects to the greater sea . . . There are predators in the sea. There must be. It's a different realm from mine, but I bet they have some equivalent to sharks or something like that. What's to stop one of those predators from coming through the tunnels and trying to make a snack of me?

It's not worth exploring.

After one last suspicious look at the tunnel, I pull myself out of the pool. The last couple days start catching up with me. Or maybe it's the life-changing orgasm I just had. I'm not prepared to think too closely about that. Not yet.

Thane doesn't like me. He may want me, but it's blatantly reluctant on his part. Really, it doesn't make any kind of sense why he even agreed to take me from Azazel in the first place. He doesn't want a kid any more than I do, apparently, and he obviously has no intention of spending time with me. I heard the emotion in his voice when he talked about his late husband. *That* is caring. What he feels for me is responsibility.

I really am doomed to repeat history over and over, aren't I?

MY LIFE FALLS into a strange new pattern over the next few days. I'm not a captive, locked away in my room, but I *am* tucked away in a mostly deserted part of the keep. Embry comes by in a hurried kind of way to drop off clothing and let me know that food will be provided to my room, but if I need anything else, I have only to ask. Ze is really nice in that genuine way that is rarer than diamonds, but ze is just as obviously far too busy for me.

That doesn't stop me from trying to keep zir with me a little longer on the second day. "Embry."

Ze pauses. Embry is Thane's sibling, and they share a lot of the same facial features, but ze is built a tiny bit leaner and zir's skin leans green, rather than blue. I think ze might be taller, but it's hard to gauge because the tentacles mean height is a relative thing. "Yes?"

"I'm bored." It comes out whiny, but it's been days, and the closest I've come to a proper conversation was some kraken-person telling me to get the fuck out of their way when I ventured down toward the kitchen. I'm trying not to take it personally, but I might as well tattoo Not Wanted on my forehead at this point.

Embry hesitates like ze wants to be anywhere but here, but zir good nature overrides zir desire to get out of this conversation. "Thane will come around."

I snort. "I think you don't know your brother that well if you think that. He doesn't want this and he doesn't want me."

"Maybe not." Embry shrugs. "But he's not a bad guy. He's given this territory everything, and that takes something from a person."

"Like their husband." A husband he obviously cared very deeply about if seeing Ramanu with a bracelet he made was enough to make Thane forget himself.

Embry gives me a disappointed look. "My brother lost the person he cared most about in the world that day. It's not a joking matter."

Ze is right, but that doesn't change the fact that I'm in this mess because he refused to let Azazel give him another human. Even if I were alone in the castle, the castle may or may not be sentient. I could be having adventures right now and annoying Azazel and getting to know Ramanu. Instead, I'm stuck in this keep where every kraken I come across looks at me like I'm fish food. "Is he going to avoid me for the full seven years?"

"No." Embry puts a tentative hand on my shoulder and

squeezes. "Thane has never shirked a responsibility once in his life, and he won't start now. He just needs some time to adjust to the whole thing."

It's obvious that Embry thinks the world of zir brother, so I'm not going to stand here and keep poking at him. That's a surefire way to get zir to leave and probably never come back, which would be even worse than the fact I perk up every time I hear tentacles against the ground, as if Thane has finally come back to finish what he started that first day.

It's never him.

Which means he thinks it was a mistake. That *I'm* a mistake.

I drag in a breath and try for a smile. "I don't suppose there's some job I could do? I'm going out of my mind here."

Ze hesitates. "You're an honored guest."

"An honored guest who's bored out of her ever-loving mind. Please, Embry. Do I have to get down on my knees and beg?"

"That won't be necessary." Ze sounds mildly panicked. "I'll see what I can do. If you really want some kind of job, I suppose there's something we could figure out. Give me a day or two."

"Thank you." I beam at zir. "I really appreciate it."

"Just . . . don't make me regret it."

"Of course. I promise."

I really hope I'm not lying through my teeth.

7

THANE

fter the encounter with Catalina, guilt chases me into the depths, and then it keeps me there for days. Revisiting the heat of her hands against my chest, the way it felt to wrap her in my tentacles, how sweet she looked as she came.

I've hardly been celibate since Brant's death. Loneliness creeps through even the hardest exteriors and drives me to seek out company. Always with the clear understanding that it will never last longer than a night, that I am incapable of giving more. Those encounters have been soft and considerate and . . . nothing like what happened with Catalina.

I wanted to bend her to my will.

I still do, if I'm being honest with myself.

"Thane." Embry descends through the entrance above me, speaking in the clicks and movements we use to communicate under the water. Ze looks about disapprovingly. "You're hiding."

"There are repairs that need to be overseen." I motion to the window overlooking the current construction. Water is a glorious element, but destructive in the way all elements are. With the keep being mostly beneath the surface, it's an ever-present battle to ensure the foundations stay strong and stable.

Embry crosses zir arms over zir chest. "Overseen personally by the leader of the territory instead of the foreman you assigned to the task a month ago."

I don't blush, but it takes effort to keep from fidgeting like a youngling caught out. Embry has always had that effect on me, for all that ze is my younger sibling. "It's an important task."

"Your human is causing problems."

"Catalina is not *my* human."

"Isn't she?" Ze cocks zir head to the side. "Because I don't believe anyone else in this territory made a deal with the bargainer-demon leader to bring a human into the territory, despite the fact you've been very clear about your desire not to breed or displace me as the heir."

I grit my teeth. "You know why I made that bargain." I had to keep our territory at least appearing on equal ground as the others. If I'm the only territory leader who didn't accept Azazel's invitation, it would have put me at a disadvantage. When things aren't equal between the territories, people get hurt.

"Yes, I do. I'm just reminding *you* of it." Embry sighs. "I know things got a bit out of control that first day."

"Excuse me?"

"Don't pull that stuffy-lord voice with me, Thane. By the time she got the courage to start exploring, your scent was *still* all over her." Zir gaze softens. "No one expects you to replace Brant."

"There *is* no replacing Brant."

"I know," ze says simply. "But Catalina is bored and she's

stirring up trouble. I don't think she means to, but she's putting some people ill at ease with her presence."

"You're not suggesting she's in danger." I narrow my eyes. "Harming the human means harming the territory." Why is my heart racing right now? Foolish question. It's because the price of failure is so high. It has nothing to do with the idea of Catalina being harmed because of my negligence. "But I hear your concern, and I will heed it. Where is she now?"

"The kitchen."

Why in Goddess's name is she in the kitchen? I don't voice the question. Embry already seems agitated enough without it seeming like I'm accusing zir of something. "Let's go."

We make it there in short order. The kitchen is one of the rooms above water for obvious reasons. Our ancestors may have existed on raw fish they hunted themselves, but my people have more varied tastes now.

I pause in the doorway and take in the disaster before me. Catalina is trying to chop . . . something. Whatever it started as, it's now mush on her board. Her face is bright red with embarrassment as the line chef, Henryk, lectures her with increasing irritation. He's a new hire but was renowned for his skill, and I have yet to see any evidence to contradict that, though the few times we've interacted have left a poor taste in my mouth.

Perhaps we should come back at a later time.

I don't think Catalina would want anyone to witness this, and I find myself reluctant to cause her further distress. Or would it be better to step in and put a stop to Henryk . . .

Even as the thought crosses my mind, his voice raises. "You're *worthless*." He waves the knife at her. Too close. Too fucking close. "Get out of my kitchen before I gut you where you stand."

I don't make a decision to move. I hear Embry's sharp

inhale behind me, and then I'm between Henryk and Catalina. "Put the knife down. Now." He *threatened* her. Pointed that blade at her fragile body and said he wanted to gut her. "Or I will put it down for you." I don't sound like myself. I sound like I want to rip his throat out with my teeth.

It's not inaccurate.

He backs up immediately, his tentacles tight to his body in fear. "Thane. I didn't know you were—"

"That should make no difference," I snarl. "Embry, have the guards get him out of here. Permanently."

"Wait, no!"

I ignore his pleas and turn to Catalina. "Go to your room and gather your things. We're leaving."

She's gone pale, her eyes too big on her face. "Um."

"Now, Catalina."

"Right. Okay. Sure." She backs up and then she's gone, darting out the door. I've scared her, but I can't think clearly enough to slow down.

The guards appear within minutes, and Embry manages the situation with far more grace and patience than I am capable of at the moment. I have to concentrate on holding perfectly still, on keeping my breathing slow and even when all I want to do is pick up that damned knife and . . .

Embry crosses to me but doesn't touch me. Smart of zir. I am shaking. Why am I shaking? "He'll be escorted from the keep. It's over."

"He threatened to gut her."

"Yes, I heard."

Ze doesn't sound particularly bothered by that, but I can't tell if it's because ze is trying to calm me or because ze honestly doesn't care that Catalina was in imminent danger.

Surely it's not the latter. Except I can't be sure. "We're leaving."

"Thane." Embry sighs. "That's an extreme solution to a temporary problem."

"No, it's really not. There are too many people here, and we cannot properly control them. Catalina is a person who incites strong emotions." I know that all too well. "If someone harms her, the entire territory will pay the price."

"Uh-huh." Embry props zir hands on zir hips. "And this has nothing to do with you being scared because she was in danger. It's only the territory."

"Of course." It feels like a lie, but I power through all the same. "I'm taking her to the tower."

Instead of looking reassured, Embry looks more concerned. "Thane, you have exactly two people on staff."

"Two people who I trust implicitly and who will not threaten to *gut* Catalina." Della and Annis are lovely ladies who have seen to my personal residence for many years. While I am not close with either, they have shown themselves to be quiet, calm, and professional at all times. "What does that have to do with anything?"

"I won't claim to know Catalina after two conversations, but she continues to seek out company." Zir concern comes from zir in waves. "If you isolate her, she may start climbing the walls."

It's a fair judgment based on my limited contact with her as well, but that changes nothing. "Better to be restless than to be harmed." There are wards on my personal residence that prevent anyone but Embry from gaining access. And Annis and Della, of course. There will be no one for Catalina to incite, and none of our enemies will be able to take advantage of this deal and harm her.

Funny how I hadn't even considered that would be a risk

until now. Henryk reacted in anger, but he spotlighted a significantly larger problem. Catalina must be contained for her safety, which means I must take her home with me.

It also means we'll be alone together.

The realization thrills me before I shut it down. My home is close enough to the keep for me to spend my days here, and I'll just sleep beneath the surface, deep enough that not even a reckless human like Catalina will come searching. She can't swim, for all that the bracelet ensures she won't drown.

It's a neat solution. "I've made my decision."

"Thane . . ." Embry shakes zir head. "Fine. Do as you will."

"It's the logical solution."

Ze doesn't answer, turning and moving out the door and away from me. Zir disapproval stings, but I'm making the best call for everyone. Catalina must be kept safe, and frankly, I must be kept from Catalina.

I don't know who that kraken was who dominated her, growled commands at her. I don't recognize him. He's not who I was with Brant, and he's certainly not the shell of a person I became after Brant's death. Better to keep apart from her and ensure he doesn't make a reappearance.

Ever.

"You want me to swim. Again."

I clench my jaw and strive to keep my patience. "You will not swim. I'll carry you."

Catalina props her hands on her hips and glares. Her earlier fear is nowhere in evidence, and I have no right to the relief that brings me. Even if it means she's challenging me. "Right, because that worked out so well last time."

She's rather magnificent tonight, clothed in a lush purple dress that hugs her torso and flares out from her hips to stop just short of the ground. One of the many I ordered on that first day. My people have little use for such garments, but humans are soft and sensitive to changes in temperature in a way we aren't. I couldn't have Catalina walking around the keep naked.

Why not?

"You said no harm was done from that experience." My voice is too harsh, an attempted escape from my wayward thoughts.

"I lied." She says it so easily, as if there was never any question of it. "I know you weren't trying to hurt me, and I wasn't going to let a little case of the bends cause you to lose your territory."

"The bends."

"Yep. Pretty sure that's what happened." She shrugs and taps her head. "I read about it once. It has to do with the pressure of being underwater. If you go too deep too fast, or come up too fast without adjusting to the pressure, your body throws a big fit."

"A big fit."

"Yes, that's what I said." A note of defensiveness creeps into her tone. "Look, I'm not a bends specialist, and I'm pretty sure I read it in a romance novel; I was more focused on getting to the naughty bits than on the science behind the bends. I don't swim and didn't anticipate it ever being a factor in my life. My mistake."

I shake my head. "It's good information to have. As I said, it won't happen again." It means spending more time during the trip with her close, but I can hardly assign

Embry to the task. Zir reaction to my decision to take Catalina to the tower means ze won't do it, and I don't trust anyone else enough to wager the territory on it.

Catalina eyes the pool I emerged from a short time ago. "And we're leaving now."

"Yes." The faster we leave, the faster I can retreat. I've only been in this room for a few minutes, but I can't escape the onslaught of memories from the last time I was here. Of how good she looked tangled up in me. Of how desperately I wanted to touch her, to taste her. I don't understand why this is happening.

Dangerous. This human is *dangerous*.

I haven't felt this kind of draw since . . .

I take a breath and force myself to finish the thought. Since Brant. But it's not the same. With him, it was as inevitable as the tide, a steady rush of needing to be close to him, to spend time with him, to get to know every part of him, body and soul.

With Catalina, it feels like a hurricane. I don't know myself when I'm with her, and she's only been in my territory for a few days.

It means I can't trust myself with her.

"Thane." From the exasperation in her tone, she's said my name more than once.

"Yes?"

She worries her bottom lip but finally says, "I think I'm afraid of the water."

"You *think* you're afraid of the water?"

"That's what I just said." She shoves back a length of her long dark hair. "I'm trying to be honest with you. There's no reason to mock me."

"I'm not mocking you." I simply do not understand how someone can *fear* the water. A healthy dose of caution is smart, but water is life. It still defies belief to think Catalina has spent her life without swimming.

She draws in a long breath, and it's my only warning before her shoulders drop and her lips curve into that wild smile. Catalina still, but more. "Really, I would think you'd be enticed by this whole experience. Helpless damsel in distress, here for you to sweep up and carry around."

"I am not enticed by incompetence." It's not what I mean to say. What I *mean* to say is that I'm not enticed by anyone but my husband, long gone and released into the depths. I've felt desire, but that's not the same thing. But once the words are out, there's no taking them back.

She's completely undaunted. "Guess you're just unlucky, then. Let's get this over with." She lifts her arms and makes a motion with her hands. "Uppies."

"*Uppies.*"

"Thane, really." She's still grinning. "How are we to communicate at all if you're just going to repeat every outrageous thing I say back to me? It makes for dull conversation."

"If I gag you, you won't be able to say anything outrageous." Once again, as soon as the words hit the air between us, I'm appalled. I never talk to *anyone* this way. Certainly not some human who's smaller and weaker than me.

But Catalina just laughs. "Always with the kinky good times. Keep making promises, and I might start to actually like you." She makes that motion with her hands again, her hazel eyes sly. "Come on, Thane. Give me uppies."

The sudden desire to have her in my arms is nearly equal to the need to put as much distance between us as possible. I have to get us to the tower, and then I can do the latter. Carrying her is just expedient. That's all.

I sweep her into my arms, slightly gratified when she

squeaks a little. I start for the pool but pause before slipping into it. "Do you know the parameters to avoid . . . the bends?"

"Um." She stares at my mouth for a long moment and gives herself a shake. "Like I said, I was reading the book for the fucky scenes, but pretty sure we're not supposed to ascend faster than thirty feet per minute. And there's a safety stop about fifteen feet below the surface where we're supposed to hang out for roughly five minutes."

I consider the information. It might not be accurate, but it's easy enough to ascend slowly and ensure she doesn't collapse again. It means more time with her in my arms, but it's a small enough price to pay. "We won't be able to communicate below the surface, but I will keep you safe."

Her smile dims. "I can't promise I won't panic." She rushes on before I can figure out something even remotely comforting to say. "But you know the old adage about panic?"

Even knowing I'm going to regret asking, I can't resist the invitation in her voice. "What old adage?"

"It's nothing a good fucking can't fix."

Her laugh cuts off as I slide into the pool and descend below the surface. It's just as well. The last thing I need to think about is *fucking* Catalina. It's bad enough that I can still feel her tightness against the tentacle I pressed into her. The arch of her spine as she came. Her breasts, plump and inviting and topped with rosy nipples. Her lips parted with desire and too overcome for that wild smile that feels like a lie.

It takes two minutes to realize the lovely flowing fabric of her dress is a hindrance. I pause and rip the bottom half of it off, leaving the fabric to float above us as we continue our descent. Someone will collect it later. The tunnels branch like hallways, though they are not confined by gravity, so I move laterally and then at an angle to reach the outer part of the keep.

From here, the sea opens around us. We're close enough to the surface that sunbeams penetrate the water, lighting the coral reef that makes up the west side of the keep, the coral extending for leagues to the north and south. Schools of fish dart about, their scales flashing pleasantly. The sight of so much open space always settles a part of me that never quite finds peace when I'm in the keep itself. Without the walls to close me in, I can breathe properly again.

Maybe that's why it takes me so long to realize Catalina isn't enjoying the view. She's made herself even smaller in my arms, tucking her knees close to her chest. She's also shaking.

She's . . . terrified.

8

CATALINA

I wouldn't call myself a particularly brave person, but I also wouldn't think the sight of so much water would fill me with the kind of fear that has me fighting to claw away from Thane and get back into the tunnels. They were claustrophobic, but at least I knew their parameters, lit as they were by strange glowing in the rock formations.

But this . . . ocean? Sea? I don't even know the proper term for it. It stretches out as far as the eye can see, the deep blue playing with my perception. Can I actually see for miles, or is it really much closer? Could there be a monster out there, all scales and teeth, just waiting for a foolish human to swim too close?

A hand under my chin gently draws my face away from the open water to look up at Thane. His hair tentacles float around his head, which might make me freak out more, but his expression is comforting in its coldness. Everything else may be different below the surface, but not this man.

He studies my face, and maybe not looking directly at the water should calm me, but I can't catch my breath. I'm *breathing underwater* and I don't think I'll ever not be awed by that. This is too much newness, too fast.

Thane says something, I think, but I hear a series of clicks I don't understand. Apparently the translation spell doesn't work with this underwater language for some reason. I shake my head helplessly. Or maybe it's my entire body shaking.

His brows draw in, and then he shifts his arm around me so that a single arm holds me, his bicep to my back, his big hand gripping my thigh closest to him. Later, I'll marvel that our size difference is enough for him to do this. I don't have time right now, not when he grips my upper thigh with his free hand, so high up that his knuckles brush my bare pussy.

The shock of the touch freezes me. My gaze flies to his face, only to find him looking at me in question. Just like that, I remember my irreverent comment before we descended.

It's nothing a good fucking can't fix.

Apparently he's decided finger fucking will be good enough for this purpose. There are a thousand reasons not to do this, but I'm not thinking of any of them right now as I stare into his inky eyes. In fact, I'm not thinking of the dangers of open water either. I hadn't been 100 percent serious before, but right now I think I might die if he doesn't keep going.

I nod jerkily. It's all the consent he needs to palm my pussy. His hands are so big that he's essentially palming my entire nether regions. I jolt as Thane starts to swim again, but I can't focus on our changing surroundings. Not when he's gently sliding his fingers through my folds.

It's not like it was before when he held me splayed out with his tentacles. That was easier to process. I challenged him, and he put me in my place with orgasms. A simple equation.

This . . . isn't.

This feels like more than conquering. It feels like *care*. Normally that would be enough to freak me the fuck out, but there's too much going on in this moment to freak out about. Being touched like this by Thane hardly ranks.

The pressure increases as we slowly descend to coast along the surface of the coral reef. Movement out of the corner of my eye makes me tense and start to whip around, but Thane chooses that moment to press a single large finger into me. He tests me for a moment, and then a second finger joins the first.

Oh fuck, that feels amazing.

The tentacles were *good*, but the hardness of his fingers, the roughness of his slow strokes, hits an entirely different kind of good. He shifts me in his arm and spreads my legs a little more, giving him better access.

And yet I can't fully give myself over to the feeling. We're moving too fast—laterally, so there's no worry about the bends—and I keep seeing things that make my mind scream in fear, sure that we're about to be eaten.

Thane shifts me higher on his chest, and then his mouth is at the corner of my jaw. His lips move against my skin, and everything goes black as one of his hair tentacles covers my eyes. I freeze, fear rising hard enough to make my head spin, but he keeps up that thorough fucking with his fingers.

My fear recedes one heartbeat at a time. Without any visual input, I only have the rhythmic movement of Thane's body as he swims, the pleasure he deals out in steady waves. Even the tentacle around my eyes is a comfort after a few moments, its weight steady and reassuring.

Thane builds my desire slowly. Distantly I'm aware that

he's drawing it out to ensure I'm distracted through the entire trip, but I don't give a damn. I'm shivering and shaking, but with need instead of terror.

Then he adds his thumb to the mix, sliding it against my clit with each slow stroke. I try to writhe, to get him to pick up his speed, to focus there, but he ignores me.

Somehow that's even better.

Pleasure builds and builds, drawn in tighter and tighter by his touch. I can't focus on anything but his hand between my thighs. I barely register that we're rising slowly and the pressure in my head is receding incrementally. I'm surprised when my head breaches the surface and the tentacle eases from my eyes.

I blink up at Thane. "Don't you dare leave me like this." I'm so close to cumming, I'm shaking.

He doesn't answer with words. His face is even more forbidding than normal as he lifts me onto the rock ledge. I get the impression I'm in a cave, and then he pushes me onto my back and unceremoniously shoves my thighs wide. This time, three fingers spear me. I cry out, my fingers scrambling over the rock as I search for something to hold on to.

Then his mouth finds my clit.

I think I forget to breathe. Surely this isn't happening. Thane doesn't like me. He was only finger fucking me to keep me from panicking and being a pain in his ass. Surely he's not licking my clit right now and making a humming noise that vibrates through my entire body.

Maybe this isn't about me at all. Maybe he just likes giving head. Or he just wants to end this and has decided his mouth is the quickest solution.

Except, once again, my body doesn't give a fuck if this is

all in my head or actually happening. I cum with a strangled scream that might be his name.

Thane presses his forehead to my stomach and gives me three more long strokes with his fingers. My orgasm scrambles my thoughts, but I still hear him say, "This is your new home now, Catalina."

Then he's gone, disappearing beneath the water with barely a ripple.

I press a shaking hand to my eyes. "Thane, king of krakens and mixed messages." That's twice now that he's delivered a soul-breaking orgasm and then fled the area. I don't know if it's shame or guilt or some misguided honor kicking in, but fuck, it stings.

I want to see the orgasms as care. Good god, I want to see them as proof that he's not as remote as he's acted since I met him. Proof that if I just try harder, he'll warm to me. It's a lie. I've gone down this road before. I've even attended enough therapy to know *why* I do it.

Poor Catalina, her mommy was neglectful to the point of abuse, now she seeks out every single unattainable partner she can find, attempting to prove she's worthy of love.

Anger and shame are a heady mixture, and they get me off my back and onto my feet. A quick look around the space shows I'm in a cavern that's half water and half stone. The walls curve up into darkness, the ceiling so high, I can't make it out. Panic has just started to lick its way up my throat when I see the dark curving staircase. It's been carved right into the wall, and there's no railing, but it's wide enough that I should be able to climb safely.

Fool that I am, I glance back at the dark pool of water. It's completely still, not a single ripple to suggest Thane has done anything but leave the premises as quickly as possible.

"A totally normal thing to do after you finger a lady and then suck on her clit until she cums screaming your name."

No one answers. Why would they? I'm entirely alone.

The thought makes me break out in goose bumps. "No. Not alone. I don't know that." Thane wouldn't do that to me. He may be cold, but he hasn't shown any evidence of being cruel. Surely he's not going to start now?

There's only one way to find out.

It takes a very long time to reach the top of the stairs. I have to take three breaks, sinking onto the stone and rubbing my shaking thighs each time. There isn't a single doorway or exit the entire time, not until I get to the very top. When I see the heavy wooden door, I almost convince myself I'm imagining it—that this staircase never ends and I'm in some hellish purgatory that will have me climbing forever as payment for some imagined sin.

Well, no need to imagine it. I've sinned plenty, at least according to the church people who have tried to save my soul periodically throughout my life. Too bad I'm not looking to be saved.

Liar.

I ignore the nasty little voice in the back of my mind and shove open the door. Or I try. It's even heavier than it looks, and it's swollen—likely from the salt air—into the doorframe. I have to shove my shoulder against the wood to even get it to budge. By the time it swings reluctantly open, I'm sweating and cursing Thane's name.

The other place wasn't so bad. Yes, the people avoided me, and there was that unfortunate incident with Henryk in the kitchen where he threatened to murder me, but at least I was dry and warm and not having to muscle my way through doors and into . . .

I look around. "Thane, I'm starting to think you hate me."

The halls and staircase seem to be carved from the same kind of stone, and I might find it beautiful if it wasn't so *damp*. I pad on bare feet across a floor that I'm pretty sure is dry but *feels* vaguely wet.

Up until this point, my outrage and adrenaline were getting me through, but it's as if reaching this hallway has the reality of this situation hitting me all at once. I'm just as damp as this hallway, my torn dress clinging to my skin and not covering the essentials. My hair is still wet and hanging down my back, my body hurts, and I'm hungry.

I search through the rooms I find, but they're all unoccupied. More than unoccupied. They give the feeling of being abandoned entirely. Just like me. With each room that I find empty of even furniture, the panicked feeling inside me grows. "Don't do this to me, Thane."

By the time I find a room that actually has furniture, I can't draw a full breath. No people. No damned people. But at least there's a bed. I slap the covers, and only a small cloud of dust rises. "Good enough."

I collapse onto the bed and close my eyes. "I can do this. It's just a little isolation. I've done this before. I can do it again."

I've lied to myself plenty of times over the years. Nature of the beast. The lies have never filled me with such hopelessness as these ones do.

It's entirely possible that I *can't* do this.

9

THANE

I t takes everything I have not to go to Catalina. Not because I seek her presence, of course. More that I want to ensure she's settling in well. There may also be a generous helping of guilt caused by Embry's words rattling about in my head.

It's almost a relief when I surface inside the keep a week later to find Ramanu waiting for me. They stand with their arms crossed and a frown pulling their lips down. "Explain why your human is behind a ward I can't cross."

A mistake. Not that I am eager to key my wards so a bargainer demon can get in, but Ramanu's check-ins are part of the ongoing contract with Azazel.

I heft myself out of the water and stare them down. "I'll rectify it by morning."

"You'll rectify it now," they snap. "If I leave here without checking on her, you're in violation of the contract."

Damn the contract, damn this demon, and damn the woman I can't stop thinking about.

I've successfully avoided going home for a week, but I

can't key the wards without being there in person. "Come along."

"I'm not swimming, Thane." Ramanu sneers delicately. "It's beneath my dignity. I'll meet you at the entrance."

I could ask them to portal me as well, but I'll need the trip to prepare myself. It would be strange if I didn't escort Ramanu to Catalina, which means I'll see her again. For the first time since I shoved her legs apart and tasted her pussy.

Desire shudders through me, and I do my best to mask the movement by slipping into the water. Goddess, her taste. The way she cried out *my* name when she came. If I didn't know better, I'd think her a witch who put a spell on me.

In fact ...

The longer I swim, the more it makes sense. Yes, that must be it. People of our realm and those of the human realm don't interact overmuch. The realms used to be easier to cross, but that hasn't been the case for generations. Still, there were those trapped on the human side when the realms closed to each other. Their bloodlines run through select humans to this day. It's entirely possible that some ancestor of Catalina's dallied with someone magic. A siren, perhaps. It'd certainly fit with the way she draws me.

I swim to the surface near my home's entrance. As promised, Ramanu stands on the small rock outcropping near the edge of the ward. They look vaguely uneasy to be surrounded by so much water with no shelter, which only serves to reinforce that they're not a fool.

The sea holds any manner of dangers, even without me or one of my people dragging an enemy into the deep.

I surge out of the water and move to the ward. "I'll need your blood."

"Naturally." They press their palm to one of their eye horns and then offer it to me.

I drag my fingers through the blood and then paint the symbol in the air in front of the ward. It's keyed to me, so it allows me to modify it so Ramanu can enter. A few seconds later, the symbol flares a deep blue. "You may come and go as you please." I glance at them. "As long as you behave yourself."

"Darling, I never behave myself." They give me a wolfish grin, but it falls away as quickly as it appears. They turn to the tower of rock in front of us. "Lonely place you have here. Why isn't she in the keep?"

Admitting I might not have my people in line is admitting weakness. It's one thing to do it with Embry, my heir. I certainly won't be sharing those details with a bargainer demon. "Privacy."

They snort. "If you say so." Without an invitation, Ramanu steps forward and through the doorway into the tower that makes up my home.

I almost turn around and leave. If not for the fact that I *can't*, I certainly would. There's absolutely no relief in the fact I must follow Ramanu through the door, that the choice is taken from my hands. I must follow Ramanu to ensure this check-in goes as it should.

We find Catalina in one of the bedrooms. She's still wearing the torn dress from last week, though she's obviously made some attempt to clean it. She's lying on a bed and twirling her hair around one finger. "So. You came back."

Ramanu takes in the room in a single sweep and spins on their heel to shove me back out the door. I allow it. I'm too shocked to do anything else. They slam the door to the bedroom and snarl at me. "What the fuck is this, kraken?"

"I don't . . ." I clear my throat. "I don't know."

"This might not have triggered the contract, but don't

play the fool with me. This is not the living conditions Azazel expects for his humans and you know it." They poke me in the chest with one long black claw. "I'm taking her out of here."

"It's fine."

We both turn to find Catalina in the doorway. She looks paler than the last time I saw her, and there are dark circles beneath her eyes. She surveys us and shakes her head. "There's no reason to fight about it. As you can see, I'm fine."

"From what I can *see*, that's not the word I would use." Ramanu has softened their tone, though. They poke me one last time. "I'm going to speak with her, and if I don't like what she says, *you're* not going to like what *I* say."

There's no time to respond, and honestly, I'm not sure what I'd say. Catalina is so clearly not okay that I don't know how to wrap my mind around it. I'm a man of action, though, and there's one action in particular I can take.

I find my staff, a young woman and an old woman, in the kitchen. They both straighten as I stalk into the room. There's a proper way to do this, but I'm too frazzled to think clearly. "What's the meaning of this? Why is Catalina still clothed in the same dress from a week ago and staying in a room covered in dust?"

The old woman, Della, frowns at me. "We're following your lead, sir. She's cast out, and so our actions reflect that."

My lead.

Goddess, I've made a mistake.

I almost snarl at them, but I know this is my fault. Not theirs. Instead I say stiffly, "Catalina is my honored guest and shall be treated as such."

Annis blanches. "I'm sorry, sir. I had no idea. If I'd known—"

"My fault," I cut in. "But see that it doesn't happen again. Have you at least been feeding her?"

"Of course." Della draws back as if struck. "We're not villains. She's been fed."

Annis leans around Della's back to look at me. "We gave her plain bread," she says helpfully.

Plain bread. Catalina has been treated as a prisoner for a week, and I had no idea, because I wasn't here. I had been so concerned about putting some distance between us—between the man I become when I'm near her—that I hadn't stopped to consider the implications.

I have no one to blame but myself.

"Put together a true meal," I grind out. "And clean another room for her, Annis." I can't blame them for the clothing situation any more than I can blame them for misunderstanding the reason I brought Catalina here. There are no clothes here that would fit a human. We only bother with cloth garments for special occasions, and even then, only the ones that won't happen underwater. It's a tradition holdover from when we interbred with humans more freely. They have strange ideas about nudity.

I head back the way I came, my thoughts already consumed by making this right. I'll have to ask Embry bring over more clothing. I'm so distracted, I almost miss Ramanu stepping into the hallway.

They don't look happier to see me than I am to see them. "She wants to stay."

"Why?" I say it before I think better of my question. I want Catalina to stay, of course. Her leaving means losing everything I've fought to make ready for Embry. It means forcing my people to submit to a bargainer demon as a leader. I do not want that outcome.

I also . . . don't want Catalina to leave.

"She has her reasons," they say shortly. They study me for a few beats. "I know you lost your husband a few years ago."

Where are they going with this? "Five years ago." So long, and yet no time at all.

"I'm sorry for your loss." They almost sound like they mean it. "No one expects you to marry the woman, Thane. Just don't treat her like a prisoner, or the next time I come here, I'm taking her back to Azazel—regardless of what protests she or you make. Do you understand me?"

"Yes," I manage. I want to hate them for the threat, but it's justified, and we both know it. "I understand."

Ramanu studies me for a little longer, then nods. "You'd better." They turn away. "I'll see myself out."

I wait until I can't hear their footsteps any longer, and then I wait a while more until the wards ping as they move through them. Only then do I turn to the closed door between me and Catalina.

Apologizing is the right thing to do. I made a serious miscalculation, and she's suffered for it. If she were anyone else, I'd already be in that room issuing my apology.

But she's not anyone else. And . . . the woman gets under my skin like no one I've ever met. I loved Brant with everything I had, until it felt like our lives merged in a way I still haven't recovered from, but he never drove me to the lengths Catalina can in just a few words.

And that's from limited interactions. Will I even be the same man if I spend more time with her? Or will the fire of her presence banish the ghosts of my past?

Ghosts I'm not ready to release. Ghosts I don't think I'll *ever* be ready to release.

Brant was the love of my life. This human woman, who I've only known a short time, cannot replace that or take that away, but that doesn't change the fact she affects me like no one else has since his death.

It scares me.

If I knock on this door, if she admits me, I don't know how the interaction will go. Will we snipe at each other? Will we manage a normal conversation? Or will she provoke me and then entice me and then disable what little control I have when I'm around her?

I can still taste her on my tongue, hear her cries of pleasure ringing in my ears. My desire puts a tremor in my hands. I want to touch her with a ferocity that borders on need. I can't guarantee I won't do exactly that if we get close again.

Because I can't guarantee it, I lower my fist and turn away from the door. Catalina's needs will be seen to. I don't need to be present to ensure it happens.

In fact, my absence will serve her further.

I turn and move away.

10

CATALINA

I t has been *weeks* since I've seen Thane. At least my treatment has changed significantly since Ramanu first arrived like a crimson wrecking ball. The food has become significantly more delicious, even if it leans heavily toward fish. Embry, Thane's sibling and heir to the territory, arrived the next day with more clothing than I know what to do with. Very little of it is practical, but that's fine.

I'm not a practical person.

Ramanu has been showing up every other day, and even though I know it's out of pity, I don't care. I'm starved for company, and their company is delightful.

Even if it's not the company I crave.

We wander the halls, and they entertain me with stories of kraken monarchs from times past. Apparently there's been some truly questionable ones. In turn, I select my most amusing life stories, strip them of anything that might be worrisome, and share those.

We stay away from the underwater passages and climb to the top of the tower, poking and prodding in every room we come across. The ones that aren't empty contain furniture even dustier than the room I made my own that first week. It couldn't be clearer that this place has been abandoned.

Fitting that Thane stuffed me here and, for all intents and purposes, appears to have forgotten me as well.

I try to make friends with the staff—Annis and Della—but they're horrified by my overtures. I can't figure out if it's because I'm human or a guest or just *me*, but they refuse to let me help with any of their tasks, and they all but run me out of the kitchen when I ask to take my meals with them.

Even with Ramanu's visits, I am . . . so alone.

I should be satisfied with the fact that I'm safe enough, clothed, and fed. If I'm lonely, I still have a better life than a lot of people have. But a locked tower isn't much better than a locked room, and I have too much time on my hands.

I go so far as to stare out my window and consider just how far I'd have to swim to escape. There are a few islands in the distance, one of which I think might be where the keep is, and an even bigger landmass that's so far away, it's barely a smudge on the horizon.

Too far. All of them, too damned far.

Even if I could swim, I would have to brave all that open space to leave. I've watched enough *Shark Week* to know just what an ocean predator can do to its prey, and I'm sure whatever these seas have to offer are so much more dangerous.

Trapped. I'm fucking *trapped*. A rat in a cage. A wolf in a trap. It doesn't matter how often I pace the perimeter or how many times I climb to the roof. There is nowhere to go.

Worst of all, I can't stop thinking about Thane.

Which is why I'm here, braving the truly over-the-top staircase to the cavern where he brought me the first day. It's dark down here and even damper than the rest of the tower. Below me, I hear water licking against stone.

Fear surges and I laugh, as if I can keep it at bay with sheer bravado. "Thane!" It's late in the day. This is obviously his home, for all that he's been avoiding the parts of it where he might run into me. He must be close.

Either that, or I'm making an even bigger fool of myself than normal.

If I had even the tiniest bit of self-preservation, I'd likely find his absence a relief. He's distant, and even though he's obviously attracted to me, he doesn't like me. He sure as hell doesn't approve of me. Also, he's half tentacles, but that's honestly the least questionable thing about him. I don't know what it says about my current state of mind that *this* is my list of priorities.

Since I've never been the cautious type, here I am, singing his name at ever-increasing pitches as I descend the stone stairs into darkness. I reach the bottom of the stairs and refuse to admit how my thighs quiver a little from the effort. I can dance all night and drink my weight in tequila, but I skip the stair machine on my infrequent trips to the gym. Even the trips to the roof aren't enough to actually build up my endurance. The thought of having to *climb* all those stairs again to get out of here makes my recklessness surge.

I'm going to feel really silly if Thane doesn't show and I have to sleep down here, but . . .

Ramanu will be gone for a while. They aren't sure how long. That's what they came today to warn me about. They're being called away on bargainer business, and they wanted to remind me that no harm can come to me but also they won't be here to keep me company. Someone else will fill in, but they'll be doing weekly check-ins, rather than coming every other day.

Alone again.

Alone always.

I look around the space. It's exactly the same as last time I was here. Aside from this small stone platform at the bottom of the stairs, the rest of the cavern is filled with water. This is where we came in, so it's obviously connected to the greater body of water.

He has to be here. He *has* to be.

"*Thane!*" My voice breaks halfway through his name. "Get up here, you fucking coward!"

Ripples form in the water and grow ever larger as they race toward where I stand. I really, really hope that's Thane and not some demon-realm predator who's about to eat me in a not-fun way. The instinct to flee almost overwhelms me, but what's being gobbled up compared to being left to wander the halls of this place alone like some ghost who hasn't had the decency to actually die yet?

Thane rises out of the water like some eldritch god, all tentacles and stern fury. I don't know what it says about me that seeing those tentacles makes my pussy pulse, but I think I can be forgiven since he's made me cum with them. Honestly, that racist white dude author got it wrong. H.P. Lovecraft didn't know what he's missing.

Tentacles are *sexy*.

So is Thane. He may be only partially humanoid, but he's well-made all the same. That look of cold disapproval on his face is all too familiar. He glares. "What are you doing down here? Did something happen?"

I refuse to see that last question as concern. *Refuse.* He doesn't like me, or he wouldn't be avoiding me. That's fine. I don't like him either. Probably.

"I'm *bored*." I prop my hands on my hips to hide my sudden tremors. "You went through a giant headache to get me, and you've risked your entire territory for the pleasure of my company. Stop ignoring me, and entertain me. Unless you want me to fuck Ramanu, which I am honestly kind of on board with because *they're* a delight to be around."

He stops at the end of the platform I am standing on and presses his giant hands to the stone as if he can't decide whether he wants to attempt patience . . . or launch himself at me like a predator wrapping around their prey. "Ramanu won't have you."

I blink. Wow. *Wow.* "Jeez, tell me how you really feel." I mean, it's not really there for me with Ramanu either. I like them a lot, but it feels more friendship and less wanting to rip their clothes off.

But that doesn't mean it feels good to hear Thane state it so baldly.

He sets his jaw. "You're mine, Catalina."

I don't feel a thrill at that sentence. Nope. Not even a little bit. "Cute, but if that's the case, I see why you don't have any pets. They'd die of neglect."

"I am not *neglectful*."

"Prove it." It's not smart to provoke him. He's proven to be caring when necessary, but despite being in his home for weeks, I don't actually know him. He might decide locking me in a tower isn't good enough and lock me in a room.

If he does that, I *will* jump out my window. Who cares if I don't know how to swim? It's not like I can drown.

"Leave," he says.

"Or what?"

He blinks those eerie black eyes at me. "Or what?"

"Yes." I'm being an asshole, but I can't stop. My tone is petulant and spoiled. If I leave, he'll go back beneath the surface, and I'll be alone again. At this point, I don't care if he yells at me as long as I don't have to be alone. "Usually there's an ultimatum or a threat involved."

Thane's fingers flex. I'm mildly horrified to watch solid stone crack in response. He speaks slowly, his dry voice somehow not echoing the same way mine does in this space. "Catalina, if you don't walk up those stairs right now, I'm going to fuck the brat right out of you."

Danger, danger, get the fuck out of here.

But I don't. This is a terrible idea. We've cum together twice before—rather, I've cum, and he's bolted like my pussy is made of acid—and he didn't have this dangerous edge to him either time. But I've never been able to resist a gauntlet thrown at my feet—usually to my detriment.

"Fuck the brat right out of me. That's a mighty big task." Part of my mind is screaming to turn around and walk away, but I already know I won't. I reach up and unclasp the shoulders of my deep purple gown. A new one, courtesy of Embry's last delivery. Ze never sticks around long enough to chat, which is somehow worse than if ze never came and the gowns just appeared in front of my door as if by magic. I liked what I'd seen of Embry, but apparently the feeling isn't mutual.

The gown slithers down my body, and Thane watches the movement as if it brings him physical pain.

I lift my chin. "Bet you can't. I'm a brat down to my very core."

I don't even register him tensing to move. One moment he's glaring at me like I kicked his dog. The next he surrounds me. Tentacles lash out, wrapping around my arms and legs and taking me to the ground with a gentleness that shouldn't surprise me but does anyway. They tighten, holding me spread wide and helpless.

Thane looms over me. I don't know why it's so terrifying and sexy that he still seems distant even while holding me down. He crosses his arms over his chest, the very picture of irritation . . . until I look into his eyes. There's nothing cold or distant there. He's staring at my body like I'm his favorite dessert and he doesn't know where he wants to start. "You are a perpetual trial, Catalina."

Tell me something I haven't heard before. "Ooooh. Big scary kraken." I don't know why I say it, other than the fact I've never known when to quit.

"Stop talking or I will gag you." Both his tone and expression are infuriatingly serious. Too serious to test him.

With a glare, I make a show of pressing my lips together. His lips twist in a smirk, and then two tentacles slither up my spread thighs toward my pussy.

I hold his gaze. This feels like the wildest game of chicken I've ever played, but I refuse to fold first. He'll do what he threatened, or he won't. Either way, I win. He didn't send me away again. Not yet. He's here, and he's touching me and giving me his full attention.

"What will it take?" He almost sounds like he's muttering to himself rather than talking to me. "More orgasms? Fucking your ass?"

"Do it," I gasp. "All of it. Now. Please."

One tentacle reaches my pussy and presses inside. I whimper in response. I'd convinced myself that I had imagined how good it felt last time, had built it up in my head until it was far too good to be real. It's soft and yet hard at the same time, and it's . . . twisting.

I'm so focused on that strange sensation, I almost miss the other tentacle pressing into my ass. It's just slippery enough to manage it, and he stops before he's gone too far. I try to keep silent. Truly, I do. But I am who I am. I gasp out a little breathy moan. "Oooh. Kinky."

"I told you, Catalina." He shakes his head slowly.

Another tentacle lashes out and winds around my head, covering my mouth. I try to curse, but he uses my open mouth to create a gag, sliding his tentacle between my teeth. He tastes slick and faintly like salt water, just like last time.

He works more and more tentacle into my pussy. The fullness is almost overwhelming—much more than the first time. I try to writhe, but I can't say if I'm trying to get away or get closer. I *hate* that he's surrounding me so effectively but hasn't put his hands on me.

"This is better," Thane muses. "You're so much more pleasant when you're like this." His tentacle twists inside of me, the fullness making me feel like I'm about to burst. It's too much. I make a muffled cry of protest, and he stops stuffing me. He doesn't retreat, though. Instead, he moves closer . . . or moves me closer to him, his tentacles shifting my body.

Pleasure beats through my blood as he looks down at me. This went sideways so quickly, and I still can't pretend I'd do anything differently. I'm sure as fuck not bored at the moment, even if I feel a bit like Thane's fuck doll. The distance between us, though less now, *kills* me.

"Touch me." The words are garbled behind the gag.

"I am touching you." He tilts me back, lifting my lower half so he can get an unobstructed view of where he's filling me. "Yes, I like you like this." His tentacle in my pussy starts pulsing in time with my racing heart. It's the tiniest of movements, but it has me bowing my back and moaning around the tentacle in my mouth. I'm so close. If he just keeps that up . . .

"Mouthy little brat." He still has that distant tone that

drives me wild, but his voice is a little rougher than normal. "You can't provoke me into fucking you. You've made this a contest of wills." He tsks. "You'll get my cock when you earn it."

I whimper. There isn't a thought in my head beyond *more, please give me more*. I'm so close, it hurts, teetering on the edge of a truly devastating orgasm. And still he watches me like I'm an interesting specimen he could take or leave. I hate it. I love it.

I start struggling. I don't know how to do anything else. It makes him pulse harder inside me, makes his tentacles wrap tighter around my limbs to keep me splayed open.

Finally, Thane presses a hand to my lower stomach. "Enough."

I freeze.

He twists his hand so his thumb can brush my clit. "Prove you can be a good girl, Catalina." His touch is so soft, I don't know if I'd be able to feel it if I weren't one giant nerve ending of anticipation right now. I think I might be sobbing. I can't be certain.

"How?"

I don't know how he understands me. Maybe he doesn't. Maybe he's simply waiting for me to lose control entirely. Thane's lips quirk in a way that's almost cruel. "Be a good girl and cum for me. Now."

I don't want to. I suddenly don't want to give Thane a single damned thing, if only to wipe the satisfied smirk off his face. Unfortunately my body has other ideas.

I orgasm. The wave rises and rises before cresting and then cresting again. When it rises the third time, I cry out in protest. Too much. It's *too fucking much*. It hits with the force of a tsunami, crashing into me and taking me under.

Sometime later, I surface to the sensation of being

carried in *humanoid* arms, not tentacles. The temptation to open my eyes is nearly overwhelming, but I'm suddenly afraid if Thane realizes I'm awake, he'll put me down and disappear again. Instead, I cuddle against his broad chest. He tightens his arms around me in response.

"I know you're back with me."

I close my eyes harder and inhale his ocean scent. This is nice, especially with the echoes of pleasure still singing through me. Thane sighs above my head and continues our ascent. All too soon he stops and sets me carefully on my feet. "Go to bed, Catalina."

At this point, keeping my eyes closed is silly, but I've never let logic dictate what I do and I'm not about to start now. "That was fun." God, I hardly sound like myself. My voice is raspy and almost weak. "We should do it again sometime. Like now."

I hear the sound of a door opening behind me, the slither of tentacles against stone. Thane takes my shoulders and turns me away from him. His cool breath brushes the shell of my ear. "If you can behave yourself for a full twenty-four hours, I'll consider it." He nudges me forward and into my room.

It's only then that I realize he hasn't actually promised anything. Only that he'll consider it. I'm in the middle of turning as the door shuts behind me. My legs try to give out, but I stumble for the door and yank it open with fumbling hands.

The hallway is empty.

Thane is gone.

Again.

11

THANE

This time, I don't leave the tower. I've tried to avoid the woman—to avoid this place—for weeks, and it took one encounter to have her wrapped up in me and cumming again.

Distance won't work.

Maybe exposure will.

Even as I reason with myself, I know I'm looking for excuses to take what I crave. I barely recognize myself in these encounters with Catalina, but for the first time in five long years, I am not thinking about the past. Instead, I'm plotting the future.

Yes, that vision of the future ends with Catalina on my cock, but it's still a change I'm not sure I welcome. Up until this point, pleasure has been something to seek in order to scratch an itch: a need like food or water or sleep. It hasn't been something I've *craved*. I never thought I'd feel that draw again, and I can't help the guilt that comes with it. Brant has been gone for years, but it feels like a betrayal to want Catalina this much.

It doesn't matter. It's inevitable.

I find Della in the kitchen first thing in the morning and relay my instructions. Perhaps I should leave again and return in twenty-four hours to enact my promise to Catalina, but there's no point to a challenge that isn't challenging. My presence seems to incite her as much as hers incites me. If she can manage to be . . . good . . . while spending the day with me, then I'll reward her tomorrow night.

Anticipation licks through me, quickly followed by guilt. I shouldn't be enjoying this woman. Her presence is something to be endured for the sake of the territory. She's not a plaything to entertain myself with.

Even as I tell myself that, I make my way up the stairs to Catalina's room. It's different than the one from Ramanu's first check-in. I had her moved to a lower part of the tower with a room better outfitted to serve her needs. If it also happens to be closer to the entrance pool, well, that's simply coincidence. The door is a bit hidden when one is climbing the stairs, so she must have missed it during her first ascent.

I knock before I can find a reason not to.

Catalina doesn't make me wait long, but when she opens the door, dark hair tumbled with sleep, clutching a robe around her, I wonder at the intelligence of this plan. She looks soft and touchable, but I must not touch her right now.

I move back. "Get dressed."

She eyes the new distance between us and rubs her face. "It hasn't been twenty-four hours." Even her sleepy voice is enticing. Goddess, but I don't understand what draws me to this woman. Why now, when I've finally settled into some semblance of normalcy?

"What is the point of a test if you're not tested?"

She brightens, and the smile she gives is so true, it takes my breath away. "You're going to spend the day with me? You mean it?"

My guilt grows, gaining layers. Guilt over letting her presence outshine the shadows of my past. Guilt for my obvious neglect. "I've ill-treated you, haven't I? Why hasn't the harm clause been enacted?"

"Oh, that. It's not harm if it's normal." She waves it away, but she won't quite meet my gaze. "I'm used to it."

Used to it.

So much encompassed in those three little words. I can't go back and change my actions in the past few weeks, but I can change them going forward.

Selfish. You want her, and you're looking for an excuse.

Yes. Yes, it's true.

"You shouldn't be used to it," I grind out.

Catalina tucks a long strand of dark hair behind her ear. "I don't suppose we can leave the tower?"

"No." I hate the way her face falls, hate even more the way she smiles to cover her disappointment. "Tomorrow," I find myself saying. "I'll take you out."

She narrows her eyes. "Is there a caveat on this offer? Are you going to tell me to be good or that I have to scrub the entire tower before I can leave?"

"Do you view both of those things as equally impossible tasks?"

"Of course." She turns and gives me a sultry look over her shoulder. "I think you'll find I'm *never* good, Thane." Catalina shuts the door in my face before I can come up with a suitable response.

It's just as well. My only response would be to drag her to me and kiss that smart mouth of hers. I shake my head slowly. I tasked her with being good, but the true challenge might be for *me* not to give in out of sheer desire.

I head to the formal dining room that hasn't been used in goddess knows how long. *Five years.* Annis waits there, her hands clasped in front of her. She squeaks a little when she sees me. "Everything will be ready soon, sir."

"Please go wait until Catalina is ready and then escort her here." I make my tone as gentle as I can, but she still jumps as if I poked her with a sharp stick.

I bite back a sigh and sink into a wide seat at the head of the table. Ever since I reached my age of majority and stepped into a leadership role within the territory, I've been achingly aware of the power imbalance between myself and my people. A power imbalance that my poor social skills only seem to exacerbate. I don't have Embry's easy charm. Ze is beloved by our people. Though they aren't exactly counting down the days until I step down, there's sure to be a celebration when I finally do.

If Azazel hadn't issued his invitation that was impossible to refuse, it would have been this year. But Embry insisted I be the one to go. Ze is still worried about me.

Embry is ready. Truth be told, ze has been ready for years. I suspect ze encouraged me to keep my position solely because ze was afraid of what I might do if I didn't have something to keep me going after Brant's death. I wish I could say ze had nothing to worry about, but my grief in that first year made me into a person I didn't recognize. I was never the most emotional person, but it was like losing him took away what little I had. I went completely numb.

It still hasn't worn off. Not entirely.

Footsteps bring me back to myself. I look up as Catalina walks into the dining room. She's somewhat tamed her hair, and she's wearing a gown similar to the one she had on last night. This time it's a pale gray, the clasps at the shoulders a pretty silver that seem to beg to be touched. To be undone.

She eyes the chair next to me and then perches awkwardly on the edge of it. Like all the chairs in this room, it's made for someone with tentacles, which means it's far too wide and sloped for a human.

"I didn't bring you here to punish you."

She looks up, startled. "What?"

"To the tower." I motion around us. I don't know why I'm doing this, but I don't know why I've done anything in this woman's presence that I have. She simply seems a bit lost, and I want to chase that look from her hazel eyes. "Henryk threatened you. I wasn't thinking. I was reacting."

"He was just angry. It really wasn't that deep."

There it is again. Her insistence that her health and well-being are somehow not worthy of note. "He had a knife."

"He didn't cut me." She shrugs. "I didn't need your interference. I would have handled it."

Just like that, I understand something that had been bothering me for weeks. "That's why the contract wasn't triggered the first day." By all rights, it should have been. We needed Embry's healing magic to save Catalina or she would have *died*. There is no other way to define that except as harm, but Azazel only knew about it because I contacted him.

"What are you talking about?"

"You expect to be hurt, so it barely registers when it happens."

Catalina flinches. "Wow, make me sound pathetic, why don't you?"

"That's not what I mean." I scrub my hand over my face. I don't want to lose my territory, but I am increasingly uncomfortable with how lackadaisical Catalina is about her safety, physical and otherwise. "Tell me what you need. I can't promise that I won't misstep, but I will do my best to ensure you're provided for."

"Pass."

"Excuse me?"

She looks around the room, obviously not wanting to meet my gaze. "I might be willing to take a pity fuck from you, but I'm doing just fine, Thane. I don't need a pity . . . whatever it is you're offering."

She's doing it again. I have to fight not to clench my fists. "I do not pity fuck."

Catalina opens her mouth, seems to reconsider what she's about to say, and twists a strand of her hair around one finger. "Okay."

"You're saying that like you don't believe me."

"Thane, you fuck me with your tentacles like you're mad at me and yourself." She holds up a hand before I can process that. "I am not complaining. That's not what this is. I just don't get the one-eighty you're pulling right now."

I don't truly understand it either, but I'm not willing to take that conversational turn with her. Being here is challenging enough, but not because I don't find myself enjoying her company. It's the guilt. There's both too much of it and not enough, and I can't begin to untangle the mess in my head. "I am trying to make things right."

"You know how you can make things right?"

I know I'm going to regret asking, but I find myself looking forward to whatever wild thing will come out of her mouth next. "I'm sure you have some suggestions."

"An orgy."

"Absolutely not." The words snap out of me like a whip.

Catalina grins at me, her eyes sparkling. "Okay, if not an orgy, then a little bit of exhibitionism. We could—"

"You will not be fucking in public, Catalina."

She pouts. "Spoilsport."

I give her a long look. She's inciting me on purpose, and we both know it, but that doesn't mean I'm unaffected by this line of conversation. I don't like the idea of her with someone else. At all. "I will not indulge this further."

"Oh, come on, Thane." She leans on the table and gives me sultry eyes. "Indulge me. I promise it will be fun."

Of that, I suddenly have no doubt. I actually reach for her with my tentacles before I catch myself and force stillness. "Be good."

Instantly, she straightens. "I'm *always* good. But I'll behave." She winks. "I couldn't possibly pass up the opportunity for your cock."

A bolt of sheer need goes through me. "Catalina," I growl.

"What?" She's the very picture of innocence. "Though I do have a few questions about the specifics." She twists her hair around her fingers again, but the move is more flirty than anxious this time. "How do you even know sex with a human will work? Do you have an octopus penis? Do octopuses *have* penises?"

"A kraken is closer to a squid than an octopus."

"You have suckers." She points at the tentacles on my head. "A *lot* of suckers."

This conversation is absurd, and yet I'm so turned on, I can barely think straight. "My people are capable of sex with humans. We always have been."

"Always have been," she echoes. Her eyes go wide. "Wait, you mean somewhere in the distant past, a human fucked a literal kraken? Not a half-human, half-kraken person, but a ship-killer giant squid kraken?"

"Yes," I say slowly.

"Wow, and I thought I was adventurous." She leans forward and eyes my lower half. "So you've fucked humans before."

"Once or twice." When I was younger and straining against my parents' rules and so sure I knew best. I almost got myself entangled with a bargainer demon as a result of playing with a human under their protection. "A long time ago." Before Embry and I became orphans in a war that ended with a whisper instead of a bang. Pointless. So much of the conflict in our realm is so incredibly pointless.

Ironic that I'm up to my eyeballs in a contract now despite escaping that one when I was young.

Catalina sits back, expression contemplative. "I'll save my next question for later because you're kind of a stick-in-the-mud and I don't think you'd consider it being *good*."

It's on the tip of my tongue to encourage her to be bad, but I bite down on the words before they can escape. What is *wrong* with me? "Why did you make your demon deal?"

"Oh. That." She dims a little, but her lips curve in that wild smile. "Money."

"Money." I frown. "You gave seven years of your life for finances?"

"People give their entire lives for money. Their health and time and energy. What's seven years?" She shrugs. "Besides, I didn't have much to hold me where I was. No reason to stay, no reason not to take advantage of Azazel's offer."

She speaks with a breezy tone that reeks of lies. I have no business demanding to know the truth . . . but I want to.

It's strange that I want to. My confusion makes my tone sharp. "There's no one to miss you?"

"That would require them to care if I'm around." She says it softly enough, I don't think she means for me to hear it.

But I do.

Goddess, I do.

Suddenly I see Catalina in a different light entirely. She's so bold and brazen and filled with light, but how many times in our short acquaintance have I wondered at the lie that is her wild smile? A mask, rather than a lie. I should have known it's a mask.

But who is the woman beneath?

I crave knowing her with an intensity that takes me aback. "Tell me about your family."

"Tell me about your husband."

I jerk back. "Excuse me?"

She doesn't move. "You heard me. If we're going to start opening old wounds, we're doing it together. Or not at all. Your choice."

Under no circumstances am I going to talk about Brant with her. It feels strange and almost like a betrayal, though I can't begin to say who I'm betraying. My long-lost love or the strangely fragile woman in front of me. I still haven't unsnarled the guilt inside me, some of which is for Brant and some for Catalina, and attempting to do it in real time will ensure I accidentally speak out of turn. "I take your point."

"I thought you might."

We both fall silent as Della and Annis come into the room, each bearing half a dozen trays of food. Too much food, for all that it smells delicious. "Thank you."

They set the trays on the table without a word and leave.

I bite back a sigh. Della still hasn't forgiven me for my sharp words after Ramanu arrived, and Annis has always been skittish around me. It doesn't look like either situation will resolve itself tonight.

"What will you do with all this money you're paying so dearly for?" A question I have no business asking, but that hasn't stopped me yet when it comes to this woman.

Catalina pokes at a plate of food with a strange look on her face. "The usual. Live a life of luxury. Eat like a queen. Surround myself with beautiful people who want to make me happy."

I frown. "Those people will only want you for your money."

"What's your point?" For once, she's not laughing. Her expression is painfully serious as she sets down her fork and looks at me. "You're the king of this territory."

"Yes," I say slowly. There's a trap here, but I can't divine the parameters of it.

"So you're the most powerful person around. Power and money are the two main things that attract people in droves. How do you know every person who cozies up to you is pure of heart?"

Something uncomfortable takes up residence in my chest. "I don't. Not until time has passed."

"Exactly. You can't tell the difference. I can't tell the difference." She picks up her fork again. "Which means the difference really doesn't matter for my purposes."

There's a wealth of information in that single sentence. I don't know what to do with it, though. Not yet. I'll need to ponder Catalina and what it is about her life that brought her to this place where she'd happily surround herself with people who don't care for her . . . just as long as they're there.

I care. I'm not entirely comfortable with the fact that I do, but I wouldn't feel this conflicted about possibly betraying Brant's memory if there weren't some genuine feelings for Catalina involved.

I'll ensure she's with someone who truly cares, even if it's only for tonight.

12

CATALINA

I'm trying so hard to be good. This is the first meal I've shared with another person in weeks, and it's like I've forgotten how to be human. More than that, I'm sharing it with *Thane*.

The conversation is awkward as we eat, mostly because I've never known when to quit and Thane is as serious as a heart attack. He takes everything I say as if it's fact, which is slightly terrifying.

I don't know if I've ever been taken seriously before.

I'm the outrageous one. Not the class clown—my mother would have locked me in a closet before she let me embarrass her in public like that—but the one who always pushes the limits with a smile on my face. I can't do that now. Not when Thane's dangled such a tempting carrot in front of my face.

I grin a little at the metaphor. I am nothing if not always on brand. *Focus, Cat.* "Thank you. For the, uh, distraction on the way here." Talking about how he made me cum all over his fingers probably doesn't fall into the realm of *good* behavior, but if I don't say something beyond commenting on the food, I'm going to burst. "I'm not normally the nervous type, but...what's the opposite of claustrophobia? I think I might have that. At least when it comes to the great open ocean or whatever."

Thane studies me as intently as he always seems to. As if every word out of my mouth is the god's honest truth. How horrifying.

Finally, he takes a long drink of his goblet. "Would you like to learn to swim, Catalina?"

No. Absolutely not. I've had my fill of water, and while it's very pretty to look at from the various windows about the tower, so is fire, and I certainly don't want to jump into the fireplace. "I'm very much in love with not drowning."

"You won't drown." He nods at the bracelet around my wrist. I probably should have taken it off once I realized the swimming trips weren't going to happen regularly, but I find the weight of it comforting. Also the fact that it means I can't drown. That's a pretty intense security blanket.

"I might get eaten."

His grin is quick and devastating. "Only if you're very, very good."

Is Thane . . . flirting with me?

This should be familiar. I flirt as easily as I breathe. But that's always been with normal people who want the normal things from me. They're entirely within the realm of expectation. Thane is not. He's so serious all the time. If he's flirting, then . . . I don't know.

I reach a shaking hand for my goblet, mostly for something to do. "As much as I'd like to sit on your face and ride until dawn, I'm more worried about whatever might be down there with sharp teeth and a hankering for human flesh."

"You have nothing to worry about. I'll be there."

As sexy as it is to think this big kraken man is going to protect me from predators in the deep, I remain unconvinced. He's bigger than me, but that doesn't mean he could take on a literal kraken. "What are you going to do? Glare at it with disapproval until it begs for mercy?"

His grin flashes again, lingering a little longer this time. "My magic is more than deterrent enough."

Magic.

I blink. "What are you, King Triton?"

His brows draw together. "Who is King Triton? He's not a territory leader in this realm."

Right. Of course. Pop culture references will fly right over his tentacled head. "He's not a real person. He's a cartoon, which is a whole bunch of drawings put together to make a figure look like it's moving and . . . You know what, never mind. It's not important." I sneak a glance at him, sure I'll see the signs of him checking out on this conversation. The glazed gaze. The fidgeting, trying to find a smooth conversational exit. Maybe even some rolled eyes at my rambling.

Thane watches me as if I'm divulging the world's secrets. His dark eyes are intent, and he's still in a way that should probably feel predatory but makes butterflies erupt in my stomach.

I lick my lips. "Um. Anyways. I'm convinced swimming will end with me as fish shit, so I would like to pass."

"Catalina." The firmness in his voice makes me shiver. "You will be here for seven years. My territory is over ninety percent water. Learning to swim is not optional."

He's probably right, but I'm stuck on something else. Obviously I knew the demon deal was for seven years; I read the contract before I signed it. But I hadn't really thought about what seven years in this tower would do to me. "I can't stay here," I burst out.

He flinches. "Unfortunately—"

"I don't mean with *you*." I don't pause to see if that's what he really intended with his statement. "I mean in this tower. Alone. Going out of my mind. It's torture, Thane." I was doing a good job of pretending I am totally fine with this setup and maybe that it's even kind of cute that he wants to protect me from chefs wielding knives, but a couple weeks have me climbing the walls. I don't like to think of what state I might be in after one year, let alone seven.

The teasing on his face disappears as if it were never there in the first place. "I intend to keep you safe."

"Keep my body safe, maybe. If you really meant to keep me mentally and emotionally safe, you wouldn't lock me up."

"You are not *locked up*." He pushes back from the table. "You are not a prisoner."

"Cool, so I can leave whenever I want." I shove back too and rise. "Guess I'll go now."

Thane rises too. "By all means, Catalina." He motions with one long-fingered hand. "Shall we?"

I'm riding high on frustration, which has never been a good emotion for me. I don't know how to deal with it, so I don't deal with it at all. Instead, I do whatever it takes to stop feeling that way. Right now, that means action.

I stalk ahead of Thane out of the room and down a damp hall. Another time, I'd lag behind so I could marvel at how smoothly he moves on his tentacles. There's a hypnotic element to the rise and fall of his body as he shadows me to the stairs. Not right now. I'm too keyed up.

It's only when I reach the bottom that I realize my

mistake. Of course, I can't leave. I can't *swim*. Which the bastard knew when he threw that gauntlet at my feet.

I spin and give a mocking slow clap. "Congratulations. You've made a fool of me. Well done, asshole."

He's obviously clenching his jaw, which I would find satisfying if I wasn't so embarrassed by marching down here. And now I have all the damned stairs to climb again.

I'm going to have an ass of steel after all this. Too bad I can't even enjoy the thought of bouncing a quarter off it right now. "I'm done," I say.

A tentacle lashes the ground in front of me, stopping me in my tracks, but when I look up to meet Thane's gaze, he's just as reserved as he always is. The only indication that he's anything less than calm is the way his tentacles shift around him.

I prop my hands on my hips and glare. "Is this the part where you shove me into the water and forcibly teach me to swim?"

Thane blanches. "That is torture."

Is it? My mother just called it learning the hard way. I learned a lot of things the hard way. I shrug. "It would get your point across."

"My *point*, Catalina, is not to torment you." He points at the water. "I will take you wherever you want to go."

"What's the catch?"

"There is no catch," he grits out.

I don't believe him. Not for a second. In the past few weeks, I've considering coming down to this pool more than a few times. All I'd have to do is jump in. As he said, I can't drown. There's no guard standing here, forcing me to stay in the tower. Only my own fear acts as my jailer.

Except that's not the truth. There *is* danger in this world, and he's as much as admitted it.

"If I tried to swim out of here without you, would I make it?"

He goes still, his tentacles freezing in place. That's answer enough, but I want to hear him say it. I hold his gaze until he shakes his head shortly. "It's possible but unlikely. There are predators in the bay that don't bother my people, but you are not one of my people."

"So. I am trapped." I don't know why he's so determined to argue with me. "A princess in a tower, except I'm no virginal innocent waiting for my Prince Charming. I guess that makes you the monster, huh?" Calling Thane a monster isn't kind, and it sure as fuck isn't smart. There's nothing stopping him from leaving me in a huff and not coming back for a few weeks.

Or a few years.

What am I going to do? I don't think the demon deal considers mental and emotional harm. How could it? It's such a nebulous thing to articulate, especially when my indicators of what really constitutes harm aren't exactly reliable. More than that, Thane isn't *trying* to hurt me. He's just being ham-handed about things.

"I want to show you something," he says abruptly.

"Okay?"

The word is barely out of my mouth when he sweeps a tentacle around my waist and slides into the water, taking me with him. The water closes over my head with a whoosh, and my instinctive need to hold my breath only lasts a moment.

I clutch the thick tentacle around me, mostly for the comfort of stability even if I have no control in this moment. Thane drags me deeper, though I distantly note that he's not going nearly as fast as he could. I expect him to head toward the opening I can see, the jagged rock tunnel illuminated by whatever plant populates the walls. Instead, he twists and takes us back toward the tower.

Well, that was a short trip.

Thane dips beneath an outcropping of rock, and later I'll appreciate how deftly he maneuvers me after him, ensuring I don't drag along the sharp-looking walls of the tunnel around us.

We emerge into light.

I blink and look around. A different type of light is in the water now. It's pale and soothing, and I'm still trying to figure out why when Thane begins his ascent. Once again, he does it slowly, though I think we can't be more than thirty feet below the surface, and the pool descends much deeper. Still, it's a level of caring I don't know how to deal with. He's still angry with me, but he's not letting his anger direct his actions.

He's not turning it on me.

We surface, and all I can do it stare. Above us is a gently spiraling opening of rock that leads directly to the sky. It's late afternoon, so the sun isn't directly overhead, but there's plenty of light to see by.

Three waterfalls pound down from various heights. The sound is strangely lovely, the rush of water constant and just loud enough that I could drown out my own thoughts if I wanted to.

The rest of the space is all rock formations that are mostly half-submerged in a handful of pools. The one we just emerged into is the deepest and obviously the only one that opens to the greater body of water. Thane carries me onto a shallow rock shelf and sets me carefully on my feet.

I turn slowly, taking in details I missed before. The overgrown patch of flowers in the center, where the sunlight must linger the longest. The openings at the top of the waterfalls that look quite a bit like doorways. The strange look on Thane's face, as if being here pains him.

The last observation gets me moving. I take a careful step toward him, and then another. He doesn't shift his tentacles out of my path but doesn't use them to hold me at a distance either. I pick my way through them until I can press my hands to his chest. "Thane . . . Why did you bring me here?"

13

THANE

I don't have an answer to Catalina's question. I haven't been to this room in five long years. It was always special to me, but after Brant was killed, I couldn't bear to be here without him. I look down at Catalina. Having her here should feel wrong. She's not Brant. She can never be Brant.

It just feels . . . different.

"This is a safe place," I finally manage. "A place I value." Her words still ring in my head. *Trapped*. I shouldn't care too much if she feels that way as long as she's safe . . . but I do care. Too much. Showing her this space won't magically make her feel less hemmed in, though. She can reach it on her own, but only if she swims. An impossible feat considering her current circumstances.

I don't know why I brought her here. There are dozens of places about the tower that would serve the purpose of a safe space for her to learn to swim. But . . . I don't regret it.

She steps carefully away from me and turns slowly to look around again. The relaxing of her body is subtle, but I've watched her closely enough to note it. Catalina inhales deeply and glances over her shoulder at me. "Well, don't just stand there like a bump on a log. Show me around."

Everything here can be seen in a single sweep, but I move closer to her all the same. "There is a hot spring there." I point to the pool tucked back between the two waterfalls closest to each other and then to the one in the middle. "This is not connected to the rest of the water by any openings big enough for predators to get through. I would like to teach you to swim here."

Catalina blinks those big eyes at me. I have no idea what's going on in that frightening brain of hers, but she keeps her wild smile tucked away. She's very serious as she examines the pool, circling it slowly. "You brought me here . . . to teach me to swim."

Her disbelief makes me straighten. "You are not comfortable in open water," I say stiffly. "This is deep enough to serve but also closed away so you can feel safe." When she keeps looking at me, I find myself continuing. "You're always safe with me, of course, but you won't be able to concentrate on swimming if you are too busy flinching at every movement around us."

She stares at me for another long moment and then nods, almost to herself. "Okay, you've convinced me. Teach me to swim."

I don't quite breathe an exhale of relief, but it's a near thing. This won't fix the overarching problem of her unhappiness here, but I don't have a solution to that problem yet. Maybe Embry will have some suggestions. Ze has been giving me sharp looks whenever ze is in my presence, so goddess only knows what opinions ze has managed to keep to zirself since Catalina arrived.

"You won't drown."

Her lips quirk into an almost smile. "Yes, I'm aware."

"I'm repeating myself because I suspect humans learn to swim very differently than my people." I reach down and touch the gills tucked just beneath my ribs. They're closed currently, since we're on land. "We learn beneath the surface."

Catalina gives that far more consideration than she's given anything else we've talked about to date. Finally, she nods. "Okay, we'll try things your way." Before I can say another word, she slips off her dress.

I should look away. I even command myself to drop my gaze. It's as if another has taken control of my body . . . specifically my eyes. I trace the sight of her. The curve of her hips, the soft line of her stomach, her breasts—goddess, but I want her. Coaxing orgasms from her, watching her lose herself to pleasure, is an addiction I don't know how to shake.

I'm not certain I want to rid myself of it.

"Thane." Catalina wets her lips. "If you don't stop looking at me like that, we're not going to swim at all, and while I'm not super opposed to cumming again, I very much want to earn your cock."

Earn your cock.

I close my eyes, but there's no relief behind my lids. Her presence soaks into every bit of this space, from the air I breathe to the rock beneath my tentacles. It's ridiculous. Absurd. One would think I'm smitten with this confusing human, which I most certainly am not. "Right."

If I don't do something quickly, I'll keep standing here staring at her, and then staring will become touching, and then she's right. We won't do any swimming at all. I'm having trouble remembering why that's a bad thing, which is problem enough.

The woman needs more than orgasms. I may not be able

to offer her proper freedom, not without accompanying her personally, but I can offer her this.

Before I can talk myself out of this route, I slide into the pool and motion for her to follow. "Come here."

Catalina doesn't hesitate. She slips into the water next to me and immediately goes under. I follow her down and catch her waist. She blinks at me, obviously trying to be calm but just as obviously not succeeding. I can't speak to her down here, but I hold her steady until she inhales deeply and relaxes.

Which is right around the time I realize I may not be the best suited to teach a human to swim. My people move with our tentacles. Humans only have two legs. But so do demons and dragons and the rest of the people in this realm. I try to remember exactly what that looks like. It's been a long time since I've had cause to swim with anyone outside my people.

I wonder if that's a mistake.

There have been so many made in the past five years. We may be at peace, but since Brant's death, it's a fraught peace. It feels more like a pile of tinder that may burst into flame at any moment. The people in different territories don't mix as much as they used to. Tensions are higher than they've been in all the years I've ruled.

None of that is a problem for right now.

I spin Catalina around until her back is to my chest. She tenses, but only for a moment. Her ass presses against me, and it's distracting, but I force myself to focus. I take her wrists and slowly move her arms in an approximation of swimming.

After brief consideration, I shift her away from me, giving her as much room as possible. She tentatively moves her arms like I showed her and then starts kicking her legs. Soon she's paddling in circles around the space. Now's the time to let go of her. She's got the idea of it, and she needs space to figure out the rest.

It's still far more difficult than it has right to be to release her. The moment I do, she sinks several feet and freezes. But when she looks up and finds me above her, she exhales a string of bubbles and begins moving again.

After ten minutes, I hook an arm around her waist and take us both to the surface. Catalina grins at me. "Did you see me? Swimming like a goddamned fish!"

She has a long way to go before anyone would mistake her awkward movements as fishlike, but I won't say a single thing to dampen her excitement. She looks so . . . happy. "You did well."

Catalina allows me to hoist her onto the edge of the pool. I realize my mistake as soon as I shift back. She's naked but for the water coating her skin, and that's more ornament than anything else. Even as I watch, a rivulet from her wet hair slides down one breast to course over her nipple. It's puckered and tight with the cool air, and I can't help licking my lips. I have barely gotten a taste of this woman, and I want so much more.

Goddess, am I really jealous of *water* right now?

She shakes out her arms, apparently oblivious to the direction of my thoughts. "Wow, that was more of a workout than I expected. Silly, right? Of course it's a workout, or it wouldn't be an Olympic sport." She lifts her legs out of the water and frowns at them. "You aren't secretly trying to get me to work out, are you? That would be shady."

I swear I don't understand half of what comes out of her mouth, but I recognize the sliver of insecurity on her face. It gives me the motivation I need to dial my desire back and focus on the conversation. "I have no desire to change anything about you."

"You'd be the first." Before I can examine *that*, she continues blithely on. "I think I've been very good, don't you, Thane?"

For once, I won't be distracted by the temptation of her desire. "Who wants to change you?"

She frowns but answers, "Who doesn't? I am hardly the perfect daughter my mother wanted, and she never hesitates to detail all the ways I've failed her as her only child. My father was distant, and when he got sick of my mom's bullshit, he took off, and it doesn't matter what I do to gain his attention, the most I get is birthday cards—usually a month or two late."

"Catalina—"

"Then there were boyfriends and girlfriends and lovers, but none of them lasted because I inevitably did something to fuck it up. I'm too much, Thane." She grins, though it doesn't reach her eyes. "So I embrace that. If I'm too much for them, they can choke on me. When I get my money from Azazel, I won't have to worry about being too much for anyone, because they'll just be happy to let me pay their way."

I want to pull her close and hug away the fragility lurking beneath her bravado. Considering the fact she's bristling and obviously ready for a fight, she might clock me in the jaw if I try. Instead, I offer her the only comfort I can. My truth. "I'm lonely, too."

"What? I didn't say I was—"

"It wasn't always like this. Before I always had Brant at my side." It hurts to talk about him, but it's not the soul-wrenching pain that first came to me with every memory. It's softened into something that aches, but better to ache than to feel nothing at all. "I think you would have liked him.

Everyone did. He was bright and shining and brought joy into every room he walked into."

Catalina watches me closely, something strange on her face. "I'm sorry you lost him."

I am, too, but that's not the point I'm trying to make. "I don't know how to be around others anymore. Not like he did. I'm too abrupt, too cold. It makes people uncomfortable." A compounded loss, though it took longer for this one to settle in. I didn't think I liked people, but I miss spending time in comfortable silence with others while I watch Brant charm the room. Without that sunshine, there is only silence, which makes people jumpy. Skittish. So I stopped trying. "Honestly, it was a bit of a relief to create space, but there are times when I miss the company."

She raises an eyebrow. "Please tell me you're not about to say we're alike."

"We aren't." I can't deny that our personalities seem to be polar opposites, but that core of loneliness is one I recognize on an intrinsic level. Maybe it's what drew me to her in the first place, though I can't be entirely sure.

"Thane," she says slowly. "You rule a territory, but even if you're right that everyone is holding their breath until you step down, that doesn't change the fact Embry clearly loves the shit out of you. It's there in every roll of zir eyes. If ze didn't care, ze wouldn't be so exasperated with you all the damn time."

I have doubted so many things since Brant died, but not that. Embry has done too much for me to doubt zir love. "People care about you."

"Do they?" She lifts a shoulder as if I can't see her emotionally bleeding out from years' worth of emotional wounds. "Empirical evidence says otherwise."

"Catalina." I wait for her to look at me. "I care about you."

"No, you don't. You don't even like me. I'm loud and obnoxious and too chaotic for your nice, orderly life. You are counting down the years until you can get rid of me."

"Catalina." I move closer and take her face in my hands. She refuses to look at me for several beats, but I'm content to wait her out. When she finally lifts her gaze to mine, I repeat, "I care about you."

"Thane ..."

She sounds like she's begging, but I can't begin to guess for what. For me to stop saying it? For me to say it more? Since I don't know, I do the only thing that I know she *will* accept. I kiss her. There's a force drawing us together that's stronger than gravity, and I am heartily tired of resisting it. I don't understand this thing growing between us, but I want it.

I want *her*.

14

CATALINA

I have thought about kissing Thane more times than I'll ever admit in the past few weeks. Almost as much as I've thought about his tentacles. His mouth. His mystery cock. The reality so far surpasses my fantasies that I don't know how to deal with it.

He holds my face between his big hands, cradling me as if I'm precious and he's afraid he'll break me. It's such a marked difference from how he's touched me up to this point, it makes my head spin.

Or maybe that's the taste of him on my tongue. I kiss him harder and slide my hands up his chest to his neck. It brings me in contact with his hair tentacles, and I hesitate. Is this not okay? They're not like snakes, but I don't know if I should be—

Thane answers my unspoken question for me, wrapping his hair tentacles around my wrists and guiding my hands to cup the back of his head. He shifts closer, wedging himself between my thighs. His larger tentacles slither up over the rock around me.

It's cool in this cave, or whatever the proper name for it

is. I don't care. I barely feel it with the heat of Thane pressing against me. His tentacles are wet from swimming, but they're cool, rather than cold. I shiver and take the kiss deeper.

He responds with a faint moan, and then his tentacles lift me, pulling me closer yet, until I feel encompassed by him. If I had the space to think clearly, I might actually believe he cares about me. He sure as hell kisses me like he does.

It's not real. I've told him—told myself—that it doesn't matter what the motivation for something is, because the result is the same regardless. I think the result of *this* will be orgasms.

Maybe a broken heart too.

No use thinking about that. No use thinking about anything at all. Not when Thane has wrapped me in himself. He shifts his hands from my face to my shoulders and nips my bottom lip. "If you want this to stop, say stop."

I might laugh if he wasn't so devastatingly serious. This isn't the time to joke. If I say "stop," he'll do exactly that, and I need him too desperately to tease him. I chase his mouth, but he stays just out of reach. "What if I don't want to stop?"

His tentacles hook the backs of my knees and jerk me down, sealing us together. And . . . holy shit . . . there is his cock, and it's as massive as he is. We're too close for me to see properly, but it feels just as human as his torso. I don't know if that's a relief or disappointment; it's hard to feel anything but pleasure with his tentacles wrapping around my limbs.

And then it moves.

I gasp. "Is your cock *prehensile?*"

"Is that a problem?"

"No. Oh god, absolutely not. Do *not* stop."

"If you don't want to stop . . ." Thane bends down, his voice rough in my ear. "Then you say *please*."

Oh god. I shiver. He hasn't *done* anything to me yet, but the promise is right there in his touch, in his voice. This time, we're not stopping. He's going to give me everything I need. "P-please."

"That's a start."

I should leave it at that. But I know myself well enough to understand I'll continue to bash myself against the cliffs surrounding his heart. The more unreachable he makes himself, the more I'll want his approval. The more I'll want *him*. The only way to combat that is to ask for nothing.

But I . . . can't.

I draw back a little and worry my bottom lip. "Thane."

He stills. "Yes?"

It would be so easy to play this safe. I almost laugh at the thought. I flew right past *safe* the moment I made the demon deal. But that was different. Azazel promised me safety, and maybe I was a fool to believe him, but I haven't had any cause to doubt his word since.

But this? This is the equivalent of putting my heart in Thane's hands and asking him not to toss it into the trash. I know how that goes. I'm never enough and yet always too much. If I couldn't make my own mother love me, how could I possibly make anyone else? Every romantic partner I've had has washed their hands of me, and Thane will as well. He has more reason to than most. I heard the sorrow in his voice when he talked about his dead husband. That was a once-in-a-lifetime romance.

How can a fuckup like me compare?

My chest lurches, and my throat tries to close. I swallow hard and try to kiss him again. Thane, being Thane, holds me back just enough that I can't make the contact that will end this conversation before it starts. "Tell me, Catalina."

I don't want to, but I know him well enough by now to recognize the stubbornness in his tone. My sigh is silent but feels like it takes all the strength from my body. We're doing this, and I have no one to blame but myself. "Don't leave. After, I mean. Don't just fuck me and then bolt like you're afraid I'm going to tie you up and shove a ring on your finger." The sudden longing for just that hits me like a rogue wave, and I have to pause to get my breath back. "If we're doing this, I want you to stay the night." There. That's a reasonable request. Isn't it?

Thane doesn't answer immediately. In fact, he's quiet long enough that I start to doubt how reasonable my request actually is. He wants me—we wouldn't be in this position if he didn't—but wanting to fuck and wanting to cuddle are two very different desires.

I almost take it back. My body throbs with thwarted desire, and I need him to make me cum, to fuck me until I can't string a single thought together. If he calls a halt to this now and takes me back to my room, I might actually die.

But it *hurts* when he leaves. I'm not naive; him staying might only mean he wants to fuck me enough to agree to the rest of it, but . . . surely I don't deserve to be so blatantly used.

If he's going to use me, the least he can do is lie to me a little to soften it.

Aren't I using him too?

I would love to say I am. That all I want are this man's tentacles and his clever hands and his stern commands to provide me with a temporary escape. It feels like a lie, though.

I'm not above lying to myself. In fact, I do it often

enough to be excellent at it. I'm just so tired of the effort it takes to shore up the fantasy.

Thane catches my chin lightly and lifts my face to his. "You want me to stay afterward."

I almost chicken out right then and there, but I've gone too far to go back now. "Yes."

He searches my eyes for a long moment and nods, almost to himself. "Very well. I don't know that my sleeping arrangements will be comfortable for you, but we can try."

Does he sleep underwater? The thought both repels and draws me, and I'm not sure how to feel. Thane doesn't give me a chance to figure it out. He kisses me again, and then his larger tentacles wrap around my wrists and guide them over my head.

He's fully supporting me now; not a single bit of my body is touching the cold stone. His tentacles writhe under me, a thick one wrapping around my waist and another two smaller ones teasing my nipples until I cry out against his mouth.

He eases me a little away from him and, god, the way he seems to drink in the sight of me, splayed open for his perusal . . . The tentacles at my nipples wrap around my breasts and squeeze a bit, as if offering them up to him. It makes my nipples tingle, and I shift, instinctively seeking friction there.

Thane reaches out and hovers a single finger over my left breast. "I like you like this."

"Like what?" I gasp. "Helpless?"

"Unguarded." He says the word almost like a musing to himself. "You can't hide when you're like this."

It's just sex. Even as I tell myself that, his words strike right into the very heart of me. "Thane—" My breath catches as he brushes the tips of his fingers over first one nipple and then the other. They're particularly sensitive from the decrease in blood flow. He has me entirely wrapped up, and yet he's barely touched me at all.

Thane's breath shivers out, and he releases one breast from his tentacle, only to palm me with one big hand. "You truly are perfectly made."

I almost argue with him. He's wrong, after all. According to so many people in my life, I'm soft in all the wrong places. My mother put me on crash diet after crash diet growing up, and when I finally drew my line in the sand at eighteen, she resigned herself to passive-aggressive comments about my weight whenever she saw me. My breasts that Thane seems so fond of prompted an ex to suggest surgery to lift them, and I have stretch marks across my hips and cellulite on my thighs. Like everything else about me, my body falls significantly short of perfection.

It's mine, so I love it out of sheer spite toward everyone who acts like I shouldn't. But it's not perfect and never will be.

"I can see you wanting to argue." Thane circles my nipple with his thumb. He has such a look of concentration on his face that my breath dies in my lungs. Each slow circle makes pleasure coil tighter low in my stomach. He hasn't even touched my pussy yet, and I have the wild thought that he may not need to in order to make me cum.

"Thane—"

"I find that I would very much like to meet whoever made you feel wanting." His voice is low and intense and . . . angry? He abruptly drops his hand, but I don't have time to mourn the loss, because he immediately circles my breast with his tentacle again. This time, he goes a step further and . . .

"Oh *shit*." The suckers on his tentacles catch my nipples,

sending deep pulses of need through me with each pull. "Thane, please."

He trails his hand lightly down my stomach, bypassing the tentacle holding me in place. "What can I say to convince you I find you perfect?"

Hard to believe you find me perfect when you leave me the first chance you get.

He must see the thought on my face. I'm having a hard time shielding my true feelings with him. I'm usually better at this. Thane stops just short of my pussy. "You don't believe me."

"You could try to fuck some self-confidence into me," I say hopefully.

"I suppose that's an option." Thane's lips curve a bit, but his eyes stay intense. "If you won't believe my words, then I'll have to show you with actions."

The words send a thrill of something almost like fear through me. I don't get a chance to argue, though, because he chooses that moment to part my pussy with his tentacles and press his thumb to my clit.

15

THANE

Catalina doesn't believe me. It's right there in her hazel eyes, in the way she won't quite meet my gaze for the first time since we met. I knew she had a painful past, of course; she's too much of a kindred spirit not to have had that. But I didn't expect to feel protective of her.

The wave of sheer rage makes me shake, and I have to close my eyes and focus on breathing for a moment. I am not particularly violent by nature. I defend my territory to the best of my ability, but my first response will never be violence if there's another course of action.

Yet I want to find whoever hurt Catalina and drag them into the deep. Hold them there until the last of their air escapes. Leave them behind for predators to find and dispose of.

The force of my feelings surprises me.

Equally surprising is how much I want to wrap her up and hold her until that lost look leaves her eyes. Until she believes she's worth fighting for. I don't understand where these impulses come from, and I feel a bit like . . .

We have a legend among my people. Long ago, we had a queen named Tatiana who fell in love with one of the Cŵn Annwn and had a child with them. Then the realms parted unexpectedly, and she was separated from her love and her child. She fell into despair and descended into the depths to mourn. She stayed there so long, her grief so strong, that the coral reef eventually overtook her, her body calcifying.

I feel like that.

Except I've awoken.

"Thane, I swear to god, if you're about to say something gentle, I might scream." Catalina's voice is ragged, her fingers digging into my tentacles. "Please don't ruin this."

I understand in that moment that she won't accept kindness from me. Not tonight. Not like this. But I know what she will accept. I take a breath and let this strange mood settle over me. I don't know what it means, or if it means anything at all. Maybe Catalina is simply the catalyst for my breaking out of unending grief. Even now it's there, lingering along the edges. I don't think it will ever go away, and part of me never wants it to.

I can give her this, though. I don't know if it's what she needs, but it's what she'll accept, and that's almost as good. "Catalina."

She presses her lips together and then seems to make a decision. She relaxes into my hold. "Yes?"

"You may be as loud as you like." I relish the surprise on her face, but only for a moment. My goal is far too close to hesitate now.

I lift her until her body is even with my chest. Then I do what I've been thinking about since the day I brought her to my tower. I press my mouth to her pussy. Her gasp is as perfect as her taste. I drag my tongue through her folds. *You taste like the sea. Like home.* Later, that thought will concern me. Right now, I need more.

There is no careful control as I feast on her. Every cry from her lips only spurs me onward. I don't know when I closed my eyes, but I try to open them, to watch her. Catalina is completely lost to the pleasure I'm giving her. She writhes among my tentacles, her body shaking and ragged sobs sounding in the air between us.

More.

I'm so hard, I can't think straight. It's a state I've become much accustomed to in the past couple of weeks. Every time I close my eyes, I see her, feel her, hear her. I've imagined this very moment more times than I want to admit.

"Thane, *please.*"

I press my forehead to her stomach and try to focus. My hands are shaking. Why are my hands shaking? "I will give you my cock, Catalina. I promise. But allow me to bring you to release first."

"I can't wait." She shifts restlessly, and it brings me far too much satisfaction to tighten my hold on her oh so briefly. To keep her legs splayed wide and her pussy available to me. It pleases me so much, I lick her again and move back up to her clit. Catalina cries out. "Your cock! Please, Thane!"

"In a moment." It's been months since my last regular bed partner. Too long. When I finally sink my cock into Catalina's wet pussy, I don't have much faith in my ability to keep myself from cumming on the spot. I'm shaking just from having her in my arms, and my cock is so hard, I'm getting a little worried about blood flow. The very least I can do is ensure she reaches completion first.

Next time will be better. Next time, I will fuck her until I feel her cum around my cock.

Next time.

I press a single finger into her. A few careful strokes, and then I wedge a second finger into her pussy. I'm not small even by my people's standards. Compared to Catalina, I'm practically a giant.

This has to be good for her. I don't want to hurt her in my eagerness.

Even so, it takes every sliver of control to maintain my position, my mouth against her clit, my fingers buried inside her, until she goes tense around me. "Thane!" Catalina's back bows, and I loosen my grip around her waist to allow it.

But only for a moment.

I need her too much to allow her to recover. In fact, it's likely better that she's still limp with pleasure as I lower her until our hips are even. Goddess, she's beautiful in every way, but especially in this moment. Her cheeks are rosy with pleasure, her eyes heavy-lidded.

I fist my cock and give myself a rough stroke. My fingers are still wet with her desire, and the scent drives me wild. Still, I manage to control myself. Barely. "Yes?"

"Now. You promised." She wets her bottom lip and meets my gaze. "Please."

I don't need further encouragement. I lift her in the air and angle my cock to her entrance. The size difference looks almost obscene, and if I hadn't been intimate with humans in the past, I would doubt she can take me. As it is, the struggle will be to take it slow, to ensure her body has time to adjust to mine. My cock is adaptable by nature, but I want to make this good for her.

"Try to relax," I murmur. After one last check of her expression, I lower her onto my cock. Slowly. Agonizingly slowly. It seems to take forever for my broad head to breach her entrance, but when it does, we both gasp. Tight. Too fucking tight. "*Catalina.*"

"I'm *trying.*" She breathes so hard, her breasts shake with each exhale. I pulse my tentacles against her nipples, increasing the suction a little, and she gasps. "Keep doing that."

I slide her down another inch. Agony. This is *agony.* I never want it to end. "You feel so good." I move my tentacles over her body, but I can't say if I'm trying to soothe her or stir her. "Let me in, Lina." I can't stop staring at her pussy, at how my cock spreads her almost obscenely.

And yet she takes me deeper yet.

I make my cock pulse inside her. Just a little bit. Testing her response.

"*Thane.*" Catalina shakes, thrashing her head back and forth. "Oh fuck, I think I'm going to cum again. You're so big and whatever you just did feels *wonderful.*" The words pour out of her without artifice or intention. "It's . . . I . . ."

I thrust, sinking the rest of the way inside her. Her eyes fly open, and she cries out. I need to slow down, need to check in, but pleasure has possessed me. It washes away all my best intentions. There is only Catalina, her pussy clamping so tight around my cock, I think I might die.

But I need her to cum again first.

I shift around so I can recline back on the rocks, bracing my hands behind me. "Look how perfect you are," I croon. I don't sound like myself. "A perfect little doll, designed for pleasure."

"Thane, *please.*"

I use my cock to feel around inside her, watching her face all the while. She's so expressive, I know the moment I found the spot inside her that will increase her pleasure. I pulse against that spot rhythmically. "Say it again."

"*Please.*"

I use my tentacles to lift her slowly, until only the head of my cock remains inside her. "Again."

Her eyes go wide when she realizes that my hands aren't even touching her. Catalina bites her lip. "I don't know if I hate this or love it."

"Do you want me to stop?"

She shivers and shakes her head. "No. Make me ride your cock. Make me take you." She whimpers, the sound so delicious, I can taste it on my tongue. "Use me like your little fuck doll. Please."

You are not a doll to be used for others' pleasure.

I don't say it. I'm the one who first called her a doll. Can I blame her for taking up the mantle and running with it? A battle to fight another day. Right now, I need to make her cum before I blow. I lower her on my cock again. "Look how sweetly you take me, little doll. Like you were made for it."

She shakes her head, but I can't tell if it's in denial or pleasure. "I hate this." She's so wet, she takes me almost easily now. Her voice is as ragged as her breathing. "I hate that you're not touching me but you're touching me everywhere."

"I'm touching you." I guide another tentacle around her waist and down toward her pussy. "Can't you feel me, little doll?"

"Yes!"

I tease her even as I lift her again. I have another stroke in me. Maybe two. I need to make this count. When I have her nearly free of my cock, I focus on stroking her clit lightly. Not enough to make her cum—not yet—but enough to have her body tensing in my tentacles. "Tell me what you need."

"You," she sobs. Her eyes are closed tight, and her body is quivering with an impending orgasm. "I just need you."

I cover her clit with the tip of my tentacle . . . positioning one of the suckers right where she needs me as I slam her down my length. The effect is instantaneous. Catalina cries out as she cums, her pussy clamping around my cock.

Oh fuck. Oh goddess. Oh—

I don't remember reaching for her. One moment I'm braced on the rock and controlling the whole encounter. The next I have my arms around her and I'm claiming her mouth in a searing kiss that feels like *she* is branding *me*.

It doesn't matter. We've gone too far to stop now. I kiss her harder as my orgasm crests. It surges . . . and then keeps going. I cling to Catalina, holding her tight as my body takes over, thrusting into her again and again. I'm vaguely aware of her now-free arms wrapped around me, her ankles locking at the small of my back, but mostly lost in the sea of pleasure.

In the end, it's everything I can do to ensure we slump onto my tentacles instead of the cold rock floor. Distantly some part of my brain is telling me that now's the time to move, but the thought can't quite take root.

Catalina shivers. "That was . . ."

"Yes."

"You were . . ."

"I know." I kiss her temple and pull her close. My cock is still half-hard inside her, but I'm not ready to withdraw. Not even when the stimulation borders on pain. "Thank you for trusting me."

"Of course." She says it like I've done a single thing to earn her trust.

Guilt rises in a slow wave. I didn't intend to make her feel unwanted, but as we discussed earlier, intent matters less than action. Than results. I did it in ignorance before, but I don't have that excuse now.

I like this woman. This kindred soul. I don't know what that means. I don't know how to deal with my heart, suddenly too present in my chest.

It's not like how things were with Brant—not in any way, shape, or form—but how long can I deny there's *something* here between Catalina and me? I don't know what to think, what to feel. Maybe that's why I speak my thoughts aloud. "I don't want to forget him."

To her credit, Catalina instantly understands. She shifts, easing off my cock, but doesn't move far. "No one is asking you to forget him." She clears her throat. "Or replace him. I know I could never do that, and I don't want to. It feels icky. You loved him very deeply. You *still* love him."

Yes, but . . . I don't like how quick she is to act as if she could never occupy that space in someone's life. In . . . my life.

Too fast. I'm moving far too fast with this, but it's as if by crossing this threshold with Catalina, I have broken free of the calcification that overtook my life with Brant's death. At least in part.

She won't thank me for saying as much, though.

"Catalina." I pull her into my arms again and shift so I'm lying on my back with her sprawled on my chest. "You are a gift beyond measure."

16

CATALINA

My first instinct is to ask Thane if he's drunk. *A gift beyond measure?* Don't make me laugh. My whole life has proved otherwise. People don't toss away priceless gifts. They cherish them. They hold them close . . . kind of like he's doing right now.

I almost push away. I actually press my hands to his broad chest and tense to do it. But I'm so incredibly tired. Tired of running from the disappointment that flavors the air of every room I walk into. Tired of trying and failing. Even tired of the hopelessness that comes with no longer trying at all.

My throat goes tight, and I swallow several times. I will *not* cry all over him as if he didn't just give me the best sex of my life. My body still sings with pleasure from how hard I came. I'll have to check later, but I'm pretty sure his tentacle-sucker things left marks on my body. I can barely wait to lie alone in my bed and trace my fingertips over them, reliving every moment of this encounter in excruciating detail.

"Are you in any pain?" Thane runs a hand down my

spine, a physical reminder that this encounter isn't over yet. I start to sit up, and his hand splays across my back as if he might hold me to him, but he releases me almost as soon as he tenses.

"No, I'm good." I'm sore, but it's a delicious kind of soreness.

"There is a healing cream the bargainer demons use with their humans. I can look into getting some if you'd like."

"I'm fine. Promise." I look down to find him watching me with an expression I've never seen on his face before. It's not cold or aloof. It's not even hot with desire. He's looking at me with something soft and almost tentative in his inky eyes.

It scares the shit out of me, but scrambling off him and diving into the water to put some distance between us is a dick move, and I don't have it in me. Instead, I look away. "I know I said a lot in the mix, but it's okay. I don't need you do to any of those things."

"Catalina."

I don't want to look at him. I'm afraid of what he'll see on my face. Being with Thane feels so good and so bad at the same time, but at least it's familiar. He's cold and I'm needy, and that dynamic is one that I've played out again and again. If he changes the game on me, I don't know how to adapt. If he's nice to me, I may fall in love with him, and that's a recipe for disaster.

Really, it's practically my brand at this point.

"Catalina, look at me." A pause. "Please."

Damn it, why did he have to say "please"? I turn back to him, a puppet on a string. He's still got that look on his face that I don't understand, but he seems to be trying to mask it, his features falling into the familiar cold, forbidding lines. Relief pulls a shaky exhale from me. "What do you want, Thane?"

He seems to consider and discard several options before he says, "I would like to spend the night with you."

My heart tries to leap right out of my chest. When it figures out that's impossible, it dives right into my stomach. God, maybe I *am* going to cry. "Thanks, but no thanks."

He doesn't move. "Are you saying that because you don't want to sleep with me . . . or because you're afraid I'm offering because I pity you?"

How *dare* he reach right into the very heart of me. I have spent so much time saying I don't give a fuck what the motivation for something is as long as the result feels good. It's the truth. It has to be.

But it feels like a lie right now.

"Catalina." Thane doesn't move, barely appears to breathe, but he feels closer all the same. "Let me hold you tonight."

Something's changed.

It can't be the sex. No matter what the romance novels I consumed by the dozens as a teenager said, sex won't make a partner fall in love with you. It won't suddenly cause someone who's saying all the wrong things—*I can't love you; I will never be with you; we can't be together*—to do a complete one-eighty.

My mother was right about that.

I don't understand, and because I don't understand, fear tries to take hold. Ironic that the fear caused by Thane's words makes me inch toward him. Seek comfort he won't give me . . .

Except he does.

The second I move toward him, he gathers me into his arms and pulls me close. It surprises a sound out of me that could be a sob. Instead of setting me away, disgusted by my endlessly messy emotions, Thane pulls me closer. He smooths my hair back and runs his hands over me, almost like he's trying to calm a wild animal.

Like he's not sure how to do this any more than I am.

"Thane," I finally manage. "I don't . . . I can't."

"Do you want to?"

Yes. More than I can say. Which is why I should move right now and get the hell away from this man who makes me feel such conflicting things. Maybe this sex didn't change things for him, *couldn't* change things for him, but I can't deny the new shakiness that permeates every part of my being. "I can't," I say again.

Now is where he'll call me difficult. He'll point out that I am fickle and as changeable as the wind, first asking to be held and then all but yelling at him when he offers exactly that. He'll realize I'm exactly as much of a nightmare to be around as everyone else has found. He'll leave.

They always leave.

Except he . . . doesn't.

Thane smooths back my hair again. He doesn't urge me to look into his eyes. He doesn't ask me again. He just pulls me closer and murmurs against my temple, "I know. It scares me, too."

I want to argue. No matter what he thinks he knows, we are not the same. If not for a tragedy, he would still be happily married to the love of his life. He may not be as beloved a leader as his sibling, but he's respected. Even I could see that during my short time in the keep. And Embry loves the hell out of him. Respect and love, two things I've chased and never quite reached; even without his husband, he has both in abundance.

But I am so damned tired. And it feels good to be held like this, as if I am valued and cared for. It's a lie. It *has* to be a lie.

I'm just not ready for the cold, hard truth.

Thane must feel me relax, because he exhales slowly in something I can almost convince myself is relief. "May I take you to bed?" A soft question. A request, not a command.

I nod against his chest. Apparently I do have some pride left, because I can't force myself to say the words, but he doesn't make me.

He gathers me close, and then we're moving, easing into the cool embrace of the water. I close my eyes. It's easier this way. To let him guide. To pretend nothing has changed.

It takes less time than I anticipated before we surface again. I shiver as warm air kisses my wet skin. That's enough to summon my curiosity, and I lift my head to look around.

We're in a room I've never seen before. Part cavern and part constructed room, it's a peaceful space. The high rock ceiling overhead has lights strung on lines in a number of directions. There are two decently sized pools tucked into one side and a massive bed that looks more like a nest, its sides curved into almost a bowl shape, on the other side. Several tables are filled with the kind of knickknacks a person collects over their life, trinkets and shells mixed in with what look to be expensive jewels.

"This is your room."

Thane's arms tighten around me. "It is." He turns us toward a small door I hadn't noticed previously. "The bathroom is through there."

I take the offered olive branch and nod. "I'll, uh, go clean up."

It's not until I'm in the bathroom with a closed door between me and Thane that I start to shake. I brace my hands on the rock countertop and let my head fall forward. "You are being ridiculous. No reason to be a baby."

The words sound horrifyingly like my mother's. I shake my head, hard. "Get your game face on, Cat. You just got your mind blown by a fucking kraken-man, and he's being nice to you. This is a good thing, not cause for alarm."

Maybe I'll believe that tomorrow. Right now, I'm feeling too raw. Ironic that all I want is to go back into the bedroom and cuddle with Thane until I feel better. Being around him is the very thing causing me this anguish, but I crave his presence all the same.

I use the toilet, take a few minutes to shower with fresh water, and then there's no reason to keep hiding in the bathroom. I check the tattoos Azazel gave me back at the beginning of this. Ramanu said something about magical birth control, and I think it's linked with the demon-bargain tattoo? I can't remember the specifics. I make a mental note to ask Thane, but the thought dies when I walk back into the room.

Thane was busy tidying up the already tidy space while I was talking myself off the edge. The strings of lights overhead are illuminated, and I'm delighted to discover they're a range of soft colors, varying from red to yellow to orange to white. They give the space a warm feel that I like a lot.

He turns as I approach, and though he's obviously trying to keep his expression locked down, he stares at me as if he's relieved I didn't crawl out a window and escape. Which is just ridiculous.

For one, there weren't any windows.

"Hey." The second I say it, I feel silly. Thane just fucked my brains out. "Hey" is the best I can do?

"I took the liberty of calling for food."

I try not to wilt at that. I don't have anything against fish, but there is a *lot* of fish in every meal I've eaten for weeks. A lady can only take so much. Still, it's nice that he thought to feed me, so I attempt a smile. "Perfect."

Thane opens his mouth, and it's everything I can do not to tense. I'm not ready to have whatever conversation lingers in his inky eyes. I don't know if I'll ever be. But he doesn't ask what I'm worrying about or talk about sleeping together again. He just motions to the short table I missed when I was taking the room in. "Do you play?"

It's a trap, but it's a good one. Choosing between a difficult conversation and literally anything else, I'll choose the latter. But I have a weakness for games. There's an intimacy that comes from playing with others, and when I once said as much, my girlfriend at the time laughed me out of the room, but I stand by it.

Reason enough to say no, but I approach anyway. "I play a lot of games. I don't know if I play this one."

His lips curve into something that's almost a smile. "I can teach you if you'd like."

"Okay." I sink into one of the two chairs available and wait for him to do the same. The curves of the chair that keep me sliding to the middle actually cradle his bottom half nicely. I jerk my gaze away before he can catch me staring, turning my attention to the board.

It's composed of squares like checkers or chess, but the colors are bit different—navy blue and pale gray. I examine the pieces laid out on my side: the gray. They almost look like chess pieces, but they're not quite the same. "This looks both familiar and not."

"According to the bargainers, it's not far off from your

chess." He explains the rules. It's so tempting to get lost in the low cadence of his voice, but I force myself to pay attention. He's right: it's pretty close to chess. The pieces look different, and the knight's movements aren't the same pattern, but most everything else is the same. They have different names than I'm used to, but it's easier to think of them in the familiar terms.

I ask a few questions about gameplay, but I have it down. "Do you play often?"

"Not anymore." He waits for me to move one of my pieces and then does the same with one of his pawns. "This set was a gift from Brant. We used to play most nights." He's not smiling anymore, but he just looks sad instead of closed off. "He would be irritated that I haven't played in far too long."

"Brant, irritated? Surely not. He seems like a saint." I don't mean to sound bitter, but it's as if I have no control over myself. I shake my head. "Sorry, that wasn't kind."

"It's okay."

We fall into an almost-comfortable silence as we play. I'm not great at chess. I never had the patience to play out a strategy. And even if I did, I wouldn't have the adaptability to abandon if it started failing. No matter how long it's been since Thane played, he's obviously very good at it, because he kicks my ass in less than a half hour.

His hand falls away from his queen, which he just moved to pin my king in place. "Would you . . . like to play again?" The hopefulness in his voice makes my heart give a worrisome lurch.

It's a lost cause. I already know it. I was going to fall for this man from the moment he set himself in my life like a tower I could never hope to scale. The fact he's giving me intimacy *now* is just the last nail in the coffin. "Yes," I say softly.

He resets the board quickly and motions for me to make the first move. It's not until I do that he says, "He wasn't perfect. Brant, I mean."

17

___

THANE

I expected it to hurt more to be back here, in the room I shared with Brant for so many years. Della has done a good job of maintaining it. When he was alive, it felt like a sanctuary from the pressing demands of leadership, but after he died, it just felt like a tomb. Everywhere I turned, there was another reminder of him and what we'd never have again.

Up until bringing Catalina here, I avoided the tower, and for the last few weeks, I've been sleeping in one of the underwater guest rooms. I didn't really think through bringing her to this room. I only wanted to show Catalina that this does mean something to me.

To give her access to something I never share with anyone.

The reminders of Brant are still there, but it's almost as if they've lost their teeth. I miss him. I don't believe I'll ever stop missing him. But instead of making me want to start swimming and never return, being here is almost like revisiting good memories.

For the first time, it feels less like a betrayal and more like a natural letting go. Not entirely. Not of everything. But of the weight I've carried since his death.

I don't know how much of that is Catalina. I watch her out of the corner of my eye as we exchange a few moves. She's still shaken. For someone who acts like nothing gets her down for long, she's got a remarkably fragile center. She's been hurt, and badly.

I hide my clenched fist in my tentacles. I can't fight the people from her past. It wouldn't fix the harm they've done, and I doubt it would make either of us feel better about our current situation.

But perhaps I can balance the scales in other ways. I draw in a breath that does nothing to steady me. "Brant was selfish."

Catalina jolts. "You don't have to do this. I know you loved—love—him."

"That's exactly it." I wait for her to meet my gaze to continue. "Someone doesn't have to be perfect to be worthy of love, Lina. Brant was charming and lovely and made my life better, but he was also selfish at times, and he could be careless with his words and the emotions of people around him." He never meant to hurt anyone, but that doesn't mean he never did. "He also never got up before noon."

"God forbid." But she smiles a little. "He sounds like a handful."

"He was." I don't know why my throat is trying to close, but I have to say the words. I *have* to. "But he's gone, and he's never coming back."

"Thane—"

"Please let me finish."

She looks troubled but finally nods. "Okay. Please continue."

"I am not looking for a replacement Brant. Such a thing is impossible and not fair to anyone." I have to look away from the hurt in her eyes. "But the past few weeks have made it clear that I've closed myself off to a lot of things, possibly in too much haste. I don't know what kind of partner I'd be. My faults are legion. But . . ." I turn back to her. "I like spending time with you. Not simply having sex, though the sex is beyond words. I like the way your energy lights up a room, Lina. I don't know what that means for the future, but I would like the chance to find out."

She picks up a piece and then sets it down again. "What happens if you decide to find out and then realize you made a mistake and don't like me at all?"

"That won't happen." I reach out slowly and cover her hand with mine. "I know you feel it too, Lina."

"No one's ever called me that." She stares at our hands. "Always 'Catalina' or 'Cat.'"

"Do you want me to stop?"

"No." She presses her lips together, and a line appears between her brows as she glares at the board. "Fine, maybe you won't decide you don't like me at all, but what happens if things go well?"

I blink. The way she says it, it's an even worse outcome than the first option. "What do you mean?"

"I'm leaving." She slips her hand from mine and moves a piece on the board. "This deal with Azazel is only for seven years, which means he's putting me back in my realm at the end of that time with a boatload of money as payment."

It's on the tip of my tongue to ask her to stay, but even I can recognize that isn't a fair request. Catalina barely knows me, and we both come with significant scars from our respective pasts. There's no guarantee we would want more than seven years together.

"What if we take it one day at a time?"

She sits back. "Don't you think that's a simplistic approach?"

She's not wrong but . . . "It strikes me that we're both prone to overthinking things and wanting surety where there is none. I like spending time with you. I think you like spending time with me as well."

"I do," she mutters.

"Then we will spend time together."

"Just like that?"

"Yes." I move my piece. "There's no rush. We have time to get to know each other. There's lots of my territory that I would like to show you." Truth be told, Embry is monarch in all but name. Ze handles the day-to-day responsibilities, and ze is the one our people go to when they have a problem. In turn, I've taken over tasks previously assigned to Embry. They're mostly tedious things, like negotiating disputes between various folks in our territory, but they leave me with quite a bit more free time than I once was accustomed to.

I've been spending those free hours wandering, but it's time to put them to better use.

"Why the change?" Catalina frowns at the board and hovers her hand over a pawn before moving it to her queen. She keeps smiling. As we play, she keeps making disparaging comments about her skill set, but she's adapted quickly to the game. She's foiled three of my strategies this time alone, and at least two of those were intentional.

After the third time, I consider my move more closely and continue the conversation. "My connection with you surprised and overwhelmed me. I tried to deny it and avoid you, but that did nothing about the connection itself, and it also did the additional duty of hurting you, which I regret."

"It's fine."

"It's not. I wish you wouldn't be so blasé about people hurting you."

Catalina appears to abandon her strategy, moving a piece at random. "It's one of those things you get used to. Most of the time, they're just being careless rather than malicious. My feelings are my own problem, or that's what my last therapist said." She makes a face. "Or maybe it was the opposite. I really don't get therapist-speak sometimes. Maybe that's why therapy never works for me."

She's talking too fast, as if she can outrun my statement. Maybe I should allow her to divert me, but I am who I am. "Weren't you the one who told me intentions matter less than the result?"

"Not me. Azazel." She shakes her head. "It was very reasonable thing to say, and I am not reasonable."

"You're very smart, Lina." I move a pawn, testing if I can draw her queen out. "You're kind and funny." I watch her consider her next move and can't help adding, "You're also so sexy, it takes my breath away."

She pauses, her hand hovering again. "You just said that to distract me from kicking your ass at this game."

"That doesn't make it less true." I find myself smiling. The expression feels strange on my face. "Did it work as far as distraction goes?"

"No," she says primly. She moves to a different piece and shifts it on the board. "Checkmate."

"What?" I jerk forward and stare at the board. Oh, the clever little brat. "You set me up."

"Did I?" Catalina bats her eyes at me, but she can't stop the broad grin from pulling at her lips. "I think it was an accident. Maybe we should play again to make sure."

This is . . . fun. I start putting the pieces back to rights. "Yes, let's."

We play long enough that the food arrives. Della delivers it herself, and I make sure to thank her profusely. It's not quite an apology for how things have gone between us in the past few weeks, but it's the first step. I'll talk to her tomorrow and ensure we're on the same page.

It's only when she leaves through the side door tucked into the wall that Catalina leans forward and inhales deeply. She goes still. "Not fish?"

"I was informed that you're getting a bit tired of the options, so I thought to try something else." I have the absurd need to fidget as Catalina pokes at the food on the plate. I find myself almost babbling. "I am on serviceable terms with Bram of the gargoyles, and so I arranged for an import of things I thought you might like."

"You did this for me?" She picks up a thick slice of bread with melted butter and some spices on it. "You didn't have to do that."

"I wanted to." Not because of guilt . . . or at least not solely out of guilt. I didn't mean to mistreat Catalina, and I can't go back and change those first few weeks, but I can ensure she is well treated going forward. If she would like to eat something besides fish, that's the least I can do. "If you want something different, all you have to do is ask."

"Surely it's not that easy." She takes a bite of the bread, and her eyes practically roll back in her head. "Whatever your reasons, thank you. This is marvelous."

My chest warms and feels strangely light. The sensation only gets more pronounced as the afternoon progresses into evening. We play a few more games, and while Catalina doesn't manage to beat me again, she's playing well enough that I have to focus in order to stay ahead of her.

But eventually she's slumping and my eyes are burning from exhaustion. I don't want to make her uncomfortable, but I'm willing to press the issue to give us both what we need: her in my bed. "Catalina."

She holds out a hand, expression mutinous. "I will come to bed with you on one condition—you don't say a single word about how fickle I am in changing my mind about this."

"You're not fickle." That, I'm sure of. She knows what she wants, but she's afraid to reach for it, even as she pretends she's not. I understand in a strange sort of way. Catalina presents a front of being as changeable as the wind, but I'm beginning to see the heart of her.

I hold out a hand. "Will you come to bed with me?"

For a moment, it seems like she might argue, but she finally slips her hand into mine and lets me pull her into my arms. "Only because you asked so nicely."

"Of course."

"No other reason. I'm just being agreeable since you fed me bread."

I hide my smile in her hair as I lift her into my arms. "I'll feed you bread every day if this is the result."

"Stop that." She snuggles closer as I ease into the bed. It's made for my people, the sides curved and the space filled with large pillows that we can burrow our tentacles around for suitable support. The result is that Catalina ends up tucked against my side, her head on my chest. She sighs. Her voice already slurs a bit with exhaustion. "If you keep doing nice things for me, I'm going to think you really like me."

I gather her closer and let her breathing smooth out in sleep before I reply, "That's the thing, Lina. I do care about you. I care about you much more than I realized."

I want to keep her.

I have six years and ten months with her. It has to be enough.

18

CATALINA

The next block of time is one of the happiest of my life. I don't even know how long it is. The days are normal enough here, but without any responsibilities to call my own, time feels fluid and insubstantial. And the nights? The nights are like a fever dream I never want to wake up from.

Thane still does have official responsibilities, but he makes time for me every day, even if only for a few games of not-chess before he takes me to bed and blows my mind seven ways to Sunday. The sex is outstanding and only seems to get more so as time goes on, but the quiet moments in the aftermath are my favorite.

The way I've found my favorite spot on his chest to cradle my cheek. How he strokes me absently as we talk, whether with a hand up and down my spine or a tentacle caressing a leg or arm. The conversations themselves, carefully curated topics that seem designed to avoid the pitfalls of my mother, my exes, and Brant.

I learn that Thane never wanted to be king, but because he was the eldest, he got the position. Not all the territories in this realm run like that, but both krakens and dragons do. In fact, for a pair of territories that seem to have the most conflict, they seem remarkably similar in a number of ways. Maybe that's why there's so much conflict. I don't know.

When Thane is able to take full days for me, he shows me new places in the territory. We start with a series of underwater caves that open into a graveyard of ships dashed on the rocks above. There are so many ships, I could spend months exploring that space and not see them all. Thane is indulgent as he swims behind me, keeping an eye out for predators as I let my curiosity run free.

There are ships that look like they came straight from a pirate movie and ones that almost look like spaceships. And everything in between. It's strangely delightful to discover how small my world really is. Maybe that would be scary for some people. I find it comforting.

Once I've exhausted my exploration of the ship grave-yard, Thane shows me an underwater . . . reverse waterfall? I don't even know what else to call it. It's beautiful and slightly terrifying, and I love it.

Today we pay a careful visit to a spot overlooking an inlet that apparently serves as the breeding ground for the dobhar chu. They're a strange mix of hound and otter, though the adults are nearly ten feet long. The babies, of course, are cute as shit. "Awww."

"They're very dangerous," Thane murmurs. "They mostly keep their hunting to these waters, but they've been known to venture out farther. If you see one, get out of the water."

I give him the look that comment deserves. Get out of the water. Right. Because there's so much land in his territory to flee to. "Sounds like if I run across one of these, I'm dead."

"No." His voice goes sharp, but then he softens it. "You're safe."

This is one of those weird arguments we still have. He wants me safe, but he can't understand there's no real safety in this world or any other. Even locking me in a tower—there's nothing to save me from falling down the stairs and breaking my neck or something equally mundane.

But I'm not going to give him shit for wanting to take care of me.

I watch the dobhar chu for a while longer, enjoying the way the babies bounce and frolic as babies of every species seem to do. They look cuddly, but I know better than to say as much a second time.

Thane doesn't rush me. He never does. He simply waits at my side for my curiosity to run out. I like that. I like *him*. We spend every night together now, and though sleeping with a man who's half tentacles was a strange experience at first, I enjoy it far too much now.

"Okay, we can go."

He sweeps me into his arms, and his tentacles make descending the cliff significantly easier than my weak-ass human hands and legs. We descend slowly, carefully. Thane glares at the water that gets closer with every second, as if daring it to produce a monster like the ones we were just observing. "We'll come back in two months when the young are old enough to start the fall migration. It's a sight to behold."

"Two months?" I blink. "Wait, how long has it been that day you taught me how to swim?"

He pauses and gives me a look. "I'm not sure. Well over a month, I think."

I go cold. *Over a month.* A month of adventures that have

been uninterrupted by my cycle. That means. . . *Oh no.* "Thane."

He must hear the fear in my voice, because he stops our descent. "What's wrong?"

I don't want to ask. I don't want to pop the bubble of happiness around us. Surely if I just close my eyes and pretend I don't know how to count, reality will kindly step away and let me continue to exist in this space.

Yeah, right.

Still, coward that I am, I close my eyes. "I should have had my period. God, I can't believe I didn't realize." I feel like the biggest fool, but I've never been all that good at tracking my cycle. Usually there's a moment where I'm sure everyone hates me and I hate myself, my body, and everyone breathing who's near me, and then a couple days later, my period starts, just like clockwork. "But that can't be right. Ramanu said something about magical birth control."

"There is a pendant that the bargainers use. I didn't think to ask for one."

A pendant. Not a tattoo. *Oh god.* I open my eyes to find Thane staring at me. I didn't realize how open he's become around me until now, when he's completely closed off. His sigh shudders out. "We'll discuss it when we get home."

Home.

Funny, but the tower *has* started to feel a bit like home. Or, if not the tower itself, then Thane's room at least. Somehow I don't feel like that will be the case after this monumental mistake.

It was only a matter of time. I should have known it was coming. Nothing good lasts forever, especially when I'm involved. I always manage to shine a light on just how much of a fuckup I am. Thane may care about me, but surely this will be the last straw for the camel's back of his patience.

We reach the surface and slip beneath it. It's almost a relief that we can't talk like this. I know Thane and the rest of the kraken can communicate underwater, but though he's tried to teach me a bit, a good portion of that communication is body language using tentacles, which I don't have. I think that's why the translation tattoo doesn't recognize it enough to work.

The return trip to the tower seems to take no time at all. Thane surfaces in his room—what's become *our* room —and sets me carefully on the rock ledge. His hands linger on my hips, but he seems to put some distance between us.

Of course he does.

Later, that will hurt. Maybe. Probably. Right now, the full clusterfuck of this situation is hitting me. I press a hand to my chest. It feels like I can't breathe, but I'm breathing. Funny how my brain can't quite comprehend that. "I can't have a baby, Thane. I *can't*."

"Okay."

I barely hear him. "You don't know what it was like growing up with my mom. I can recognize that she was a monster in her own way now, but there's some damage I just can't undo no matter how hard I try. If I have a baby, I'll just be passing on that generational trauma."

"Catalina—"

"I *can't*."

"Lina, look at me." He catches me gently by my shoulders. "Generational trauma does not make you more or less worthy of being a parent." He tightens his grip slightly. "But if you don't want children, no one is going to make you have a baby."

"But the contract—"

"Fuck the contract." He pauses and seems to try to

temper his tone. "This is your choice, and if Azazel or anyone else thinks they can force your hand, I'll kill them."

I blink, my panic skidding off the rails. "You can't just murder someone on my behalf."

"I promised to keep you safe."

"But . . ." Why am I arguing? I don't know. I don't know anything anymore. "But if you have a baby with a human, that will benefit your territory."

"Fuck my territory." His hands tighten briefly on my shoulders again. "You are not a pawn, Lina. You're not a womb to be utilized or a body to be used for others' benefits. You are a person, and you get to choose what you want."

He's saying all the right things. Why does it hurt so much? "You'll resent me no matter what I do."

He shakes his head slowly. "No. I never intended to have children, but if you are with child and want to keep it, I will celebrate with you. If you are pregnant and don't wish to be, I will go to Ramanu and discuss our options. My people have ways of dealing with such circumstances, but you're human, and I won't give you anything that might harm you."

"Just like that," I say faintly. My choice, and he'll support me either way. "I'm sorry, Thane. I didn't mean for this to happen."

"It took two of us to get here." Shame flashes across his face. "I should have discussed protection with you and ensured you were taken care of that way. I'm sorry."

Despite everything, I laugh a little. "Trust us to be the only two people falling all over ourselves to apologize and take responsibility for this kind of thing."

He smiles a little. "It is incredibly typical of us, isn't it?"

I pull in a breath, and it almost feels like my lungs fill all the way despite what feels like an invisible band wrapped around them. No blame. He's not accusing me of anything or being shitty. He's simply giving me the choice to do what *I* need. I can do this. I know I can do this. "Please contact Ramanu."

Thane nods. "Consider it done."

I expect him to dive back beneath the water, but he moves deeper into the room. I watch him dig through a chest that looks like it was pulled from some ancient wreckage a million years ago. He finally straightens with a small mirror in his hand.

I lean forward, expecting some magical something or other, but Thane just taps a finger against it until I'm ready to scream at the sound. Just when I'm about to tell him to knock it off before I break the damned thing over his head, there's a shift in the air and Ramanu pops into existence.

They curse and prop their hands on their hips. "You know, there are less annoying ways to get my attention."

"I couldn't risk you ignoring them." Thane sounds as cold and distant as he did on the day I met him. "We need your assistance."

"We . . ." Ramanu turns and focuses on me. They start to grin, but the expression falls right off their face. I can't be certain, since they don't have eyes and all, but I'm pretty sure they're focusing on my lower abdomen. "Someone's been busy."

"I want it gone," I blurt.

Ramanu opens their mouth, but Thane speaks first. "Think carefully before you start quoting the contract at us, demon. Forcing her to keep a pregnancy she doesn't want is harm."

"No shit." They look absolutely disgusted. "I don't know how they do things in this territory, but we would never force anyone to go through that." They cross to me and take my hands curiously gently for the anger I can practically feel emanating from them. "Is this what you want?" they ask, so low that I have to strain to hear. "It's your choice. Not his."

Against all reason, I'm trying not to cry again. I've liked Ramanu since I met them, but I'm used to their cutting wit and irreverent attitude. This soft caring makes me feel wobbly, like the ground has shifted beneath my feet. "I want it gone," I repeat.

"Okay." They squeeze my hands, taking me at my word. "I have to retrieve someone who knows more about this sort of thing, and she'll see you through the process." They squeeze my hands again. "It will be quick and painless. I promise."

"Thank you," I say, voice thick.

With a faint pop that I feel more than hear, they're gone, leaving me alone with Thane again. He moves closer but looks like he's not sure if he should give me space or try to comfort me. A few weeks ago, I would have retreated, but . . . "Thane?"

"Yes, Lina?" He lifts his hands and then lets them drop back to his sides.

I drag in a breath, and then another. "I would really like you to hold me right now if that's okay."

He's at my side in an instant, pulling me into his arms and hugging me tight. "I will be there with you the entire time. No harm will come to you. I promise."

I bury my face in his chest and cling to him. I have no doubts this is the right call to make, but I'm already mourning the way it's going to change our relationship.

How can it not?

19

THANE

I've almost calmed myself by the time Ramanu reappears in the room. Of course, them arriving with a strange human woman in tow erases all the work I've done to ensure I'm as collected as possible. I pull Catalina closer on instinct, and she gives a sad little laugh that makes my chest ache.

"It's okay." She pats my chest.

It's not okay. I don't point out that I could feel her shaking the entire time I held her. I certainly don't ask her again if she wants to do this. She'll take it as me putting my feelings forward, and I don't want her to think I'm willing to do anything but support her in this.

I fucked up. There's no other way to look at it. It's been so long since I was with someone for any length of time, and I'm so used to magical pendants preventing pregnancy that I never bothered to ask if Catalina had a human version in place. It never even occurred to me.

Fool.

Selfish, damned fool.

Ramanu guides the woman toward us with a hand on her back. "This is Lenora. She'll get you sorted, love."

Lenora gives me a sharp look, and I have to fight not to hold Catalina even closer. Either I trust Ramanu to ensure this is done, or I don't. I don't think they're out to commit harm against Catalina, but I don't know this stranger. "Who are you?" I ask.

"I just said—"

The woman raises her hand, cutting Ramanu off. She's got lightly tanned skin that might be from the sun or genetics, long dark hair, and sharp features. She also has an aura of magic around her that almost seems to bite at the air. Dangerous.

She holds my gaze. "I'm a witch, and I know more about this sort of thing than you do, so release the girl, and she and I are going to have a nice little conversation, and then if it's what she wants, I will walk you both through the steps."

Catalina pats my chest again. "It's okay," she repeats.

Letting her go is the hardest thing I've done in a very long time. I want to keep her wrapped up, but I helped put her in this position, and I can't protect her without help. Goddess, I really am a fool.

I'm tense as I watch Lenora and Catalina move just out of earshot. Lenora doesn't exactly go soft, but she's clearly taking care with Catalina as they speak. I'm grateful for that, even if I don't like this witch much.

"How did this happen?"

I glance at Ramanu. "I don't think I should have to explain the biology of it."

"Not that." They swipe a hand over their bare skull. "There are dozens of birth control options. Why didn't you request one for her?"

Shame heats my skin. "It didn't occur to me."

"It didn't . . ." They shake their head sharply. "Azazel would rip your heart right out of your chest if you said such a foolish thing to him. I highly suggest you don't." They look back at the women. "I should have been here. If I'd realized you were fucking, I would have suggested it myself."

I don't ask where they were. I saw the way they touched Lenora, and they have what looks like a binding mark on their arm. There's a story there, but I honestly couldn't care less about it. Not in this moment. "There have been a lot of missteps with this situation, but the blame lays solely with me."

"Yes, well, make it right." They hesitate. "You're shit at the soft stuff, Thane. Unless something's changed in the past few weeks, I suggest you let me take her back to the castle while she recovers. She's going to be a bit raw emotionally, even if it's just with relief, and if you open your mouth and say some foolish shit, you're going to hurt her."

"I would cut my own heart out of my chest before I hurt her."

Their mouth works for a few beats, but no sound comes out. Ramanu clears their throat. "Things really have progressed between you two."

"Okay, this is how it's going to work." Lenora approaches again, an arm around her shoulders. She keeps her voice soft as she speaks to Catalina. "I have a potion that will do the trick, as well as a secondary one to ensure you're comfortable. A little magic will help it along. Any questions?"

"How fast can you make the potion?" Catalina asks.

Lenora shares a look with Ramanu. "Give them a few minutes to collect my things, and we'll start immediately."

Catalina's shoulders slump. "Good. I want this done."

"Of course, honey. We'll get it done." Lenora gives me a

sharp look. "And you, don't say anything that makes me want to hex you."

I expected the worry and guilt. I didn't expect the fear that rises in a wave I can't escape. I know what this sort of thing requires from one of my people, but humans are a different story altogether. I've almost forgotten how small Catalina is compared to the rest of us. Surely it's so much easier to break her. To do something that meant she wouldn't wake up afterward. "How dangerous is this?"

"No more dangerous than most other medical procedures." Lenora shrugs. "Less dangerous than childbirth itself."

People die in childbirth. Even with all the magic we have at our disposal. It's something I've always taken as fact. Now I want to rail at the goddess herself for the risks involved. "Have you done this before? Because if not, I'll go find someone more capable. Catalina deserves the best, and—"

I can't lose her.

"Don't insult me. I like the darker arts, but I'm a trained midwife, and this goes with the territory." Lenora turns to where Ramanu has reappeared again, a bag in their hands. The brown satchel seems too small to contain whatever is necessary for this, but the witch takes it with a soft smile. "Thanks."

"I threw in a few extra things you might need."

"Good." She rolls up her sleeves. "Let's get started."

In the end, it goes just as smoothly as Lenora promised. As best I can tell, Catalina sleeps through the entire thing. I'm glad for it. I sit next to her and clutch her limp hand and watch the witch like a shark. It's everything I can do not to pepper her with questions about the process, but I don't want to do anything to put Catalina at risk, and that includes distracting Lenora.

"She'll be waking up soon." Magic sizzles in the air, making my nose burn, and all evidence of the procedure vanishes. Lenora weaves a little. "Damn, teleportation magic never gets easier. I'm still woozy from coming in."

"I could have done it for you." Ramanu loops an arm around her waist and tucks her against their side. "Sit down. I'll get the bottles ready."

"Thanks."

After they're done, Lenora sets a pair of bottles on the nearest table, along with a small earthenware cup. "If there's any lingering pain." She points to the first one. "Half a cup, no more." Next, the second bottle. "For sleep, as needed. Again, no more than half a cup. They're safe to take at the same time, so don't worry about overdoing it as long as you stick to the dosage. I'll be back in a few days to check on her, but if there's excessive bleeding or if she goes lethargic and unresponsive, contact me at once."

It's hard to speak past the fear that spikes in response to her words. I thought we'd be out of the danger zone, but apparently that's not the case. "Is that likely?"

Her expression softens a little. "Not likely, but still something to watch for. Everything went smoothly." She hesitates but finally shakes her head. "Look, people react to this sort of thing differently. Some cry. Some don't. Sometimes there's guilt or shame or whatever the fuck. Sometimes there's just relief." She must see my confusion, because she points a sharp black fingernail at me. "My point is that no matter how she reacts, it's the right way for her, and *your* only job is to be there and be supportive."

"I do support her."

"Supportive does *not* mean fucking her brains out unless that's something she wants to do and feels ready for. Even if she says she's ready, you should wait a week, likely more."

I jerk back. "After all this, *that's* what you think I'm prior-
itizing? Don't insult me."

"Good. Then we have nothing to worry about." She
glances at Catalina and then at Ramanu. "Should we stay
until she wakes up?"

The demon's watching me, their mouth pulled into a
tight line that I can't read. "No, I think Thane has it from
here. Don't you, Thane?"

I don't know that I have anything at all, but I will do
whatever it takes to ensure Catalina gets what she needs.
Whatever that looks like. In fact . . . The first whisper of a
plan takes root in my mind. A way to make this right, once
and for all. It hurts to even consider losing Catalina, but I
can't pretend I don't deserve hurt after how poorly I've
mismanaged this entire situation. "I have it covered."

"Good." Ramanu's tone is still unreadable. They offer
their hand to Lenora. "Let's go."

She hesitates, but after one last look at Catalina, Lenora
slips her hand into Ramanu's, and they teleport out.

Then there's nothing to distract me from Catalina
herself. I stroke her knuckles with my thumb, over and over,
measuring the cadence of her breath. Inhale. Exhale. The
faintest movement of her chest. Is she too pale? There was
some blood, but I have no frame of reference for if it was too
much or the expected amount. Lenora hadn't seemed
concerned.

She is fine.

She is breathing.

She will be okay.

"I'm sorry," I murmur. "I've mishandled this from the
beginning. I don't know how the contract hasn't been triggered at this point, because there's no point in pretending
you weren't harmed by my actions and words."

She keeps sleeping peacefully. My gaze travels to her stomach, and I don't know what I expected to feel, but all that's present is relief that her need was met. Children are not . . . There's nothing *wrong* with children, but I've never had a burning desire to have any of my own. I meant what I said—I would have supported Catalina in whatever choice she made—but I feel no loss.

I'm just happy she's okay. I haven't lost *her*.

Yet.

Her hand twitches in mine. "Thane?" Her voice is hoarse, but when her eyes flutter open, it's the most beautiful sight I've ever seen. "It's done?"

"It's done."

She smiles a little, though it doesn't reach her eyes. "I'm sorry."

"You have nothing to apologize for. I'm the one who—"

"If I have nothing to apologize for, then neither do you." She closes her eyes again. "Did they leave?"

"They thought you might prefer a quiet recovery." I reach for the first bottle with a tentacle. "Are you in pain?"

"Only a little." She opens her eyes and watches me pour the correct dosage into the cup. "I'm mostly tired."

"Drink this, and then you can sleep." I glance at the bed and then away. As much as I want to hold her right now, this isn't about my needs. It's about what she needs. "If you want me to take you up to your old room, I can do that."

"Thane." She accepts the cup with hands that shake a little. "You're doing the noble-sacrifice thing, and I don't have the energy to navigate it right now, so I'm going to be blunt. I'm shaky and don't know what to feel beyond relief, so I would greatly appreciate it if you'd hold me tonight."

"Of course." Do I sound too eager? I'm not sure I care.

After Catalina takes the dosage, I help her to the bathroom and allow her to chase me out of it. I don't go far, though. She seems steadier on her feet, but that doesn't mean she won't fall. Again and again, I can't shake the feeling that I've botched this beyond all reason. Maybe she doesn't see it that way in this moment, but I know she will as soon as she gets some distance.

I . . . want her to stay.

Not for the night. Not even for the seven years. Forever. I haven't felt this kind of connection with anyone since Brant, and while it's very much different than what I felt for my late husband, it's no less strong.

But my desires have little to do with what's right for her.

There is the territory to consider as well. I can't officially step down from leadership of the territory until the demon deal is finished. It would put my people in danger, would make us look weak. Embry is more than capable of leading —ze is doing it in everything but name already—but ze doesn't have a human partner, which means ze doesn't have the promise of a potential half-human child to keep people in line. To keep all the territories on even ground.

If I were putting my territory first, I would have insisted Catalina keep the pregnancy.

The thought makes me sick to my stomach. If I weren't king, there's a decent chance Brant would still be alive. I am heartily tired of others paying the price of a position given to me by birth.

I know I should wait, should let Catalina rest and recover, and be nothing but a silent support for her, but I can't quite manage it. As soon as we're in bed and she's back in my arms, I say the thing that's been plaguing me since the procedure. "Do you want to go home?"

20

CATALINA

I'm so exhausted, I almost convince myself that I didn't hear Thane correctly. "What?"

"I know it's only been a few months, but I have already caused you harm several times, and we both know it. Even if the contract hasn't acknowledged it because *you* refuse to acknowledge it, Azazel will if we take this to him."

I turn to face him. Thane looks tormented, his expression stormy and vulnerable. That last bit is enough for me to check my instinctive emotional response to what feels like rejection. Thane and I have already proven we aren't always on the same wavelength when it comes to communication. I will not jump to conclusions.

I *will not.*

"If you break the contract, you lose your territory," I finally say.

"So be it." He says it so bluntly, as if he's really willing to let his whole territory pay the price of our foolishness.

I believe him. I swallow hard. "Thane, don't be ridiculous. Even if there was harm committed—and the contract

hasn't pinged it, so why would we bring it to Azazel's attention?—you're still weighing one person against thousands.
Those don't balance out."

"You know, that's what Embry told me when I wanted to
go to war after Brant died. Sol claimed it was an isolated
incident, committed by one of the old dragons who felt
Brant trespassed on their territory. Not an act of war. Something to be dealt with quickly and quietly so we don't ruffle
the tentative peace between our peoples." He's not looking
at me anymore. "Ze was right, but it doesn't change the fact I
am heartily tired of sacrificing the people I care most about
in the world for the greater good."

My heart can't decide if it wants to drop or beat itself
right out of my chest. "Embry would tell you the same thing
in this situation that ze did before."

"I'm aware." Thane's arms and tentacles tighten around
me, but he's careful not to hold me too hard, and he stays
well away from my stomach. "I don't care. I'll sign away the
leadership to Embry. I should have done it after Brant died.
Once I do, the contract is null and void on that end."

I'm pretty sure Azazel won't think so, but it's obvious this
argument won't make him see reason. *He's trying to send me
away.* My inner child wails at the thought, making it hard to
think, but I have to. We're poised on the edge of a blade, and
one wrong move will send us hurtling into actions we can't
take back. "Do you want me to leave?"

He jolts. "What kind of question is that?"

"One I need an answer to."

He drags in a breath. "I have hurt you."

He knows I have nothing to go back to, and he still
thinks he's the worse option. *"Thane."* My patience spins out,
nearly snapping. "That is not an answer, and I'm going to

need you to stop flogging yourself with guilt. Do you want me to stay or not?"

"Of course I want you to stay!" He flexes around me as if fighting his desire to plaster me to him. "I love you. But that means less than nothing because I don't know how to be in a relationship anymore. I am too blunt, and I constantly do things that hurt you even when I'm trying not to." He finally looks down at me, inky eyes devastated. "I don't know how to be anything other than what I am, and the last thing I want is to cause you pain. I don't see a way through this."

It feels like I'm being split in two. Part of me wants to cling to the harsh things, to the fact he is trying to send me home and that's just proof he's like everyone else who thought I wasn't good enough. The rest of me is fighting tooth and nail to keep my mouth shut while I process everything he just said.

He loves me.

He doesn't want to hurt me.

He doubts his ability to be good enough ... just like I do.

I press my hands to his chest and sit up so I can see him properly. "Thane ... I think we're already in a relationship."

He blinks. "Excuse me?"

"I've been sharing your bed for weeks." I speak slowly, feeling my way through. "We see each other every day. We go places together, and you show me things you care about. Maybe we aren't always the best at communicating because of our respective baggage, but that's something we've already made progress on, don't you think?"

He blinks again. "I suppose ..."

That gives me the courage to keep speaking. "Don't you think, given more time, we might learn to communicate even better? If we're both willing to try?" When he doesn't immediately respond, I take my heart in both hands and propel myself into a leap of faith. "I love you, too. It crept up on me, but it's the truth. I know when we first met, I said I didn't care about the motivations of the people in my life as long as the results felt good, but you've shown me there's no substitute for being with someone who actually cares about me."

"Catalina." He reaches up and cups my face with one big hand. "I don't deserve your grace."

"That's the thing about grace. It's not about deserving." I cover his hand with mine and give a choked laugh. "For fuck's sake, you're about to give up your territory for me. I don't know of a bigger grand gesture than something like that. How can you say you're not good for me, Thane?"

He searches my face. "I will give up my territory." He must see my panic, because he rushes on. "Not to Azazel. But it's long since time for Embry to take over. Ze is practically running the place these days."

"You don't have to do that." I can barely comprehend the sacrifice he's making. "Not for me."

Thane smiles slowly, and the expression lights up his face. "I'm doing it for both of us." He looks around the room. "Maybe we could move somewhere smaller. Farther from the keep. Into one of the villages on the coast."

"Do you really mean it?" I whisper.

"Yes." He kisses my forehead. "I'll talk with Embry tomorrow." He kisses my brow and then my nose. "But you don't have to decide about staying now, Lina. We have time to pursue this properly." His lips brush mine. "Allow me to court you the way you were meant to be courted."

The thought thrills me. "Yes."

"Good." He kisses me lightly and then urges me down to lie on his chest. "Now rest. It's been a long day."

The events of the past few hours crash over me. I brace, waiting for shame or guilt or something, but there's just a deep sense of relief. I made my choice, and I have no regrets. I have more hope for the future than I ever could have dreamed.

A future with Thane.

I'm smiling against his chest as sleep finally takes me.

I WAKE up to the sound of Thane and Embry speaking in low voices. I can't quite see them from my position, but I hear them clearly enough.

"Are you sure?"

Thane huffs out a laugh. "I should have passed it over years ago, and you know it. It's time."

"But the contract. Catalina. All of it. It's dependent on you holding the leadership position. You're *good* at leading." Embry doesn't exactly sound like ze wants to convince Thane not to step down, more like ze wants to ensure he isn't doing it for the wrong reasons.

"I'm not what we need now. You are." Thane's voice warms. "It always should have been you."

Ze snorts. "I see you're serious, so I won't keep questioning it. If this is truly what you want, then I'm happy for you." Ze hesitates. "But if she'd stayed pregnant . . ."

"That's enough." He doesn't snap, but there's no give. "I'm done letting people I love be hurt for the sake of the territory. If you would like a human partner, you're more than welcome to approach Azazel and make your own contract."

"Maybe I will."

I don't have siblings, but even I recognize the stubborn lilt to zir voice. I don't know if ze will actually do it, but Thane could probably egg zir into it the way older siblings always seem to manage.

Of course, he doesn't. "Thank you, Embry. I know this hasn't been easy to balance in the past five years, and I doubt I'd still be here without you holding me in place."

"You would have recovered just fine," ze snaps. "You just needed a kick in the ass." Zir tone warms. "Catalina is quite the kick in the ass, isn't she?"

"Yes." He's smiling. I can hear it in his voice. "Now, she's been through a lot, so it's best you leave before she wakes."

"So nurturing," Embry teases. "You're such a softy when you're in love. I'm happy for you, Thane. Truly."

"Thank you. I'll be available for anything you need during the transition of power, but I think we both know you're the leader in all but name right now, so I don't expect much friction."

"Stay well."

"You, too."

Then Embry is gone, with only a faint sound to indicate ze slipped into the water. I feel Thane approach more than I hear him, and I open my eyes as he stops next to the bed. He smiles a little. "You heard all that?"

"I didn't expect you to move so fast with resigning."

"It was time." He shrugs and eyes me. "How are you feeling?"

That's the question, isn't it? I wet my lips, trying for honesty instead of humor. "I'm sore and feeling a little brittle, but I'm relieved. No regrets."

"Okay." His shoulders dip a little in something like relief of his own. "Embry brought some food, and if you're up for it, I thought maybe we could play for a bit."

My chest feels like it's expanding, my heart growing to a truly absurd size. "Is there bread in that meal?"

His grin is wide and happy. "Of course."

"You have yourself a deal."

EPILOGUE
CATALINA

Three weeks later, we send Della and Annis to new positions in the keep and move into a new home. It's on one of the small outskirt islands that pepper the sea Thane's people call home. There's only a single entrance— at Thane's insistence for security reasons—and it's deep below the surface. The tunnel leads up into a space that's remarkably like his private rooms in the tower. The walls curve upward to a high ceiling that he has lighting installed in. There is a full kitchen with plenty of small windows that overlook the coast.

My favorite part, though, is the bedroom. The whole ceiling is open to the sky above—warded and shielded, of course, so the elements don't actually get in. I can lie in our bed and watch the stars, which brings me more joy than I could have ever anticipated.

Thane brings me more joy too. We still stumble over communication regularly, but we've both learned to pause a conversation before it spirals out of control. Most of the time. It's amazing to be with someone I feel safe enough with, someone I can navigate bumps with, without being afraid he will drop me like yesterday's trash because I'm not perfect. We're already growing together, and it makes me downright giddy to think of spending years and years with him.

And today we're taking our relationship to a new level.

"Are you sure I look okay?"

"You look amazing." Thane takes my hand and lifts me out of the water. I haven't been back to the keep since that first week, and I can't help a little thrill of anxiety.

Today, he presents me to the kraken court.

Embry has taken over as monarch, and apparently the transition of power is finished. Ze really was doing a lot of it already, so it was more a formality than anything.

Thane squeezes my hand. I don't think he's stopped smiling since that morning when things changed with us forever. It's as if he's set down a burden he was carrying for a very long time. He even talks about Brant more now, though sometimes emotion chokes his voice. I can't say I entirely understand, because I've never loved and lost the way he has, but I don't expect it's the kind of thing that ever really disappears.

It makes me value what we have all the more. Not a replacement for his husband. Just ... different.

We move through the corridors. Up ahead, I hear voices speaking in low tones. It's almost time.

I tug on Thane's hand until he stops and looks down at me. "Change of heart?"

"What? No. Nothing like that." I drag in a breath. "But I want you to promise me something."

He's oh so serious as he says. "Of course. Anything."

God, but what did I do to deserve this man? Some days it still feels like it will be snatched from my hands. But I trust

Thane. And . . . I trust myself. I manage a smile. "After this, I would like a reward."

"A . . . reward."

We haven't had sex in three weeks. First because I needed time to heal physically, and then because I felt too raw emotionally. Even with the new birth control pendant that hangs around my neck, I had to work through my feelings.

I'm ready now.

"Yes, a reward. I think I've been a very good girl." I step closer to him, and he parts his tentacles to allow it. "So when we get home, I would very much like you to rip this dress right off me and do your best to fuck the brat out of me."

The smile drops off Thane's face, leaving only naked heat. "You're sure."

"Very sure."

He searches my face for several beats and nods slowly. "Very well, Lina. Be good while I introduce you to all the politicians and very important people in the next room . . . and then I'll drag you into the nearest supply closet and fuck you until you can't remember your own name."

The breath leaves my body in a whoosh. "How am I supposed to focus with *that* happening in the near future?"

Thane's grin goes sharp. "I suppose you'll find a way, won't you?"

"I love you." The words burst out of me, too strong to contain.

He pulls me into his arms and kisses me hard. "I love you, too. Now, let's get this over with so we can have some fun." He takes my hand, and we turn to walk through the door. Meeting the court side by side. Together.

With Thane at my side, I'll never have to face down

scary experiences alone again. I'll never be *alone* again. I don't know what I've done to deserve this, but maybe he's right when he says it's not about deserving good things as much as it's about accepting them when they come.

We're both doing better with that sort of thing these days.

"Hey," I whisper. I wait for him to look down at me. "I love you."

"You just said that." He tugs me a little closer. "Say it again."

"I love you, Thane. Now and forever."

THANK you so much for reading The Kraken's Sacrifice! If you enjoyed the book, please consider leaving a review.

If you want to know what Ramanu was up to during that time away, you can check out their story in The Demon's Bargain, available on KU now!

Made in the USA
Columbia, SC
20 December 2024

50022562R00109